THE PORTUGUESE PRINCESS

TIBOR DERY

THE PORTUGUESE PRINCESS

and other Stories

Translated by
KATHLEEN SZASZ

QUADRANGLE BOOKS
CHICAGO

CONTENTS

A CHARMING OLD GENTLEMAN

A CHARMING OLD GENTLEMAN

THE coral coloured dusk poured in through the bars of the kitchen window, the lower, cobwebbed half of which was sunk below ground-level. The lawn spread all the way up to the bars; looking out one could see the dancing blades of grass and the finely chased calyxes of the daisies and the yellow wolf's milk from below. The kitchen was a narrow, whitewashed room but at this time of the day, towards evening, it sparkled like a jewel box in the green and purple light of the sunset.

Inside, a little peasant girl with a red kerchief on her head squatted in front of the range blowing at the embers with all her might. It was quiet in there, only the dry branches crackled in the range and a long way off one could, at times, make out the trams jangling at the Zugliget terminal.

'He is a good, decent man, my husband is . . .' said Aunt Anna who was sitting in a corner watching the fire. 'Just imagine, child, he's had nothing but a cup of coffee and some bread for supper for the last three years. Coffee and bread, that's what an old man needs, I told him three years ago, the last time he upset his stomach. And ever since . . .'

The little peasant girl's eyes flashed in the joyous light of the dancing flames and tears sparkled under her lashes from the smoke. The flames threw luminous yellow waves on the whitewashed walls that seemed to carry the whole kitchen on their backs.

Aunt Anna took the coffee herself to the gardener's lodge, to the small, mouldy, earth-smelling room in which she and her

husband had lived since May. After supper, Uncle Miko rose
and set out for his constitutional walk. The evening breeze
which had been bending the daises in front of the cobwebbed
kitchen window and blowing smoke into Mariska's large dark
eyes, now whipped gustily round the tails of Uncle Miko's
morning coat, pushing the small, refined, grey haired gentleman along before it. After ten minutes of half walking, half
flying, Uncle Miko turned into the Green Hunter restaurant.

'The usual?' asked the waiter wiping the table onto which
the big chestnut tree had dropped a few shrivelled leaves left
over from last autumn.

'That's it, my boy,' said Uncle Miko with a gentle smile
pulling out his handkerchief and carefully polishing his spectacles. The waiter brought him a stewed sirloin steak, with
fried onions on a tin dish. The old gentleman gazed at it
happily for a few moments and then, obviously to prevent it
from growing cold, he devoured it with miraculous rapidity,
in two minutes flat. He had a delicate little mouth and tiny,
healthy rodent's teeth. Not a crumb of food got caught in his
grey goatee. He had started on the cheese and was sipping his
second glass of beer when his daughter Marta came up quietly
and stopped at his table.

In her shocked face, petrified with surprise, a little smile
lurked under the skin, ready to rise to the surface. It played
round her flashing white teeth and in the concealed fine lines
round the corners of her mouth, but in this first minute it
could not break through the thick veil of amazement and
fright.

The old gentleman rose and kissed his daughter's hand
ceremoniously. The young woman was still trying to get her
breath back when the waiter put a wine glass before her. The
old gentleman poured out the wine with one hand and pushed
the menu towards her with the other, his wrinkled features
turned with tender solicitude towards her young face.

'Be my guest, my darling,' he said spreading his arms with an elegant, courteous gesture. 'Did you come in here by chance, or did you see me through the fence?'

An hour later father and daughter were walking hand in hand, singing, along the moonlit Szarvasko lane, at the end of which stood the villa of the old gentleman's son-in-law. When they left the restaurant the gipsy band had played a flourish in their honour.

'Aren't you tired, dear?' Uncle Miko asked. 'Shall I order a taxi? You look so enchanting tonight that I shall stand under your window and serenade you until morning.'

'Aren't you afraid my husband will come out and thrash you?' Marta asked laughing. 'You go on home, or mother will start worrying and have another of her migraines. I have to go home too, I only dropped in to see you for half an hour.'

Uncle Miko kissed his daughter's hand, then he walked up and down the alley under her window. His small, fragile body with the fluttering coat-tails threw a birdshaped, graceful shadow in the moonlight; whenever he pulled out his hand-kerchief to wipe his glasses, that, too, began to flutter in the wind, making the whole apparition as light as if it were going to soar suddenly up to the roof. An acacia tree wrapped Uncle Miko in a sweet, nocturnal cloud of scent. The old gentleman began to sway with happiness; surreptitiously, lest anybody see, he wiped a tear away from the corner of his eye. His white beard turned even whiter from the chestnut petals shaken down on his head by the wind.

Life is beautiful, thought Uncle Miko. He crushed the leaf of a walnut tree between his fingers, then stroked his beard with it so that it, too, should smell elegantly of spring. The grasshoppers around him played better even than the gipsies.

It was six months ago, in the holy week of Christmas, that

Uncle Miko had last embezzled a small sum of money at the Kobanya Cotton Mill and, though his sons-in-law had paid up, he was, naturally, dismissed from his job. In the course of the last ten years, ever since he had lost his wealth and was compelled to take a job, several irregularities of this or a similar kind had disturbed the even and enjoyable tenor of his life. His well-to-do sons-in-law had always saved him, and if they were indignant it was not so much because of these recurrent irregularities but because of the old gentleman's polite but adamant determination to earn his own bread. He was, however, no less persistent in embezzling any money on which he could lay hands. After the mishap at the Kobanya Cotton Mill his sons-in-law found him a new job only when the old gentleman threatened to commit suicide and did not come home for two days to his sick wife who was suffering from kidney, liver, and gallbladder. Aunt Anna lay in bed unconscious for twenty four hours.

Uncle Miko had started work as a book-keeper with a paper wholesaler in Sas street in the first days of April. His first month's salary was spent in two weeks and in May he paid for his sirloin steaks, his Eau de Cologne with which he sprayed his beard, and his elegant pig-skin spring gloves with the money he had acquired early in May by a lucky stroke of business. The details of this transaction were uncovered on the very same day when he played host to his daughter at the Green Hunter.

'Mr Miko, you have forgotten to hand in the receipt for eighty pengoes from the paper transport company,' said the director, a short, fat gentleman with a head so bald and pink that his whole person seemed naked in its light. A round piece of black adhesive plaster, the size of a fly, sat in the middle of the bald pate. Uncle Miko thought it was a fly and was repeatedly tempted to swat it.

'How could I hand in the receipt,' he said smiling gently,

'when I have not paid in the money? Where there is no payment, there is no receipt.'

'And why was there no payment?' asked the director and his pate turned a dark, congested red.

Uncle Miko shrugged politely, in almost imperceptible contempt.

'I borrowed that small sum of money,' he said mildly. 'I had just run out of change.'

There was silence, only the director's panting could be heard. Uncle Miko's shortsighted eyes peered at the fly that had still not left the director's head.

'How did the money come into your hands?' asked the director quietly.

'Oh, very simply,' replied Uncle Miko. 'Hasn't Janos told you?'

He threw a kindly, conspiratorial glance at the office boy who was standing at the opposite end of the desk wringing his cap in embarrassment, while heavy drops of sweat ran down his forehead.

'Come on, Janos,' he said heartily, 'you don't have anything to be ashamed of, it wasn't you who made a mistake!'

Janos groaned and wiped his forehead with the back of his hand.

'This is a very intelligent and honest boy,' Uncle Miko said to the director and his right hand swung forward involuntarily to chase the fly off his boss's head. 'I heard that the accountancy department was sending Janos to the paper transport people, and as my son-in-law, Istvan Bohunszky, retired forestry councillor, lives in the same building, No. 12, Honved Street, and I had intended to pay him a visit anyway, I told Janos to go and have his dinner, I'd take the money for him.'

'You blasted idiot!' said the director to Janos. 'How dare you hand over money that was entrusted to you?'

Uncle Miko's gentle, childishly bright face sagged. He snatched his glasses from his nose and held them up high in the air.

'I will thank you not to call this boy an idiot!' he cried indignantly and his grey goatie shook.

Uncle Miko spent the following morning in the Museum Park; he didn't have the heart to inform his sick wife of this new mishap. On another bench he caught sight of Janos, who rose, clicked his heels, and politely lifted his hat. The old gentleman noted with surprise that instead of his uniform cap the lad was wearing a hat.

'They've sacked me, too, sir,' Janos admitted shamefacedly when Uncle Miko questioned him. 'It won't be easy to get a new job,' he sighed.

'They sacked you?' Uncle Miko asked.

Janos nodded.

They sat side by side silently in the sunshine. Children were playing around them in the garden and a young girl in red was helping an old man to walk along the path. Once she caressed his blue-veined hand hanging helpless by his side. Uncle Miko rose.

'I shall put this right,' he said. 'Wait for me here, my boy.'

He had never been so angry in all his life. He lifted his gentle old hand and slapped the director who had deprived an innocent boy of his daily bread and refused to take him back; then, his glasses broken, his beard tousled, the tails of his morning coat fluttering in the wind, he reappeared in the Museum Park half an hour later.

'Let us go and have a glass of beer, my boy,' he said to Janos.

They sat in a little beer-garden near the Market. On the red-covered table the beer sparkled with snowy foam on top and drops of icy sweat were running down the sides of the glass. It was long past lunch-time, a lone lorry-driver sat in the garden next to the entrance. After a while the man rested his head on his arm and fell asleep in the misty heat.

'It's a hard life,' said Uncle Miko spreading out his arms in an elegant gesture. 'Hard for those who are honest. I could own a carriage and horses, if only . . .'

'Sure,' said Janos quietly.

'My wife, poor woman, is sick,' Uncle Miko sighed. 'I don't know how her heart will stand up to being told that you were dismissed.'

Janos's face clouded over. 'Don't tell her, sir.'

Uncle Miko ordered more beer, they sipped in silence. There was no sound except the sharp, loud ringing of the streetcar on Vamhaz Avenue. To Uncle Miko, who was dreaming of his carriage and horses of forty years ago, the sound appeared out of place.

He sighed deeply.

'Don't worry, sir,' Janos said comfortingly, then he hit the table with the flat of his hand. 'We are young and strong, aren't we, now?'

'True enough, son,' Uncle Miko nodded. 'But how could they have done this to you!'

The brilliant sunshine retreated slowly from the garden. 'Nothing is lost,' said Uncle Miko and now it was he who brought his small white fist down on the table. 'My sons-in-law will get you as many jobs as you want!'

They sat in the beer-garden until evening, mostly without speaking. At times Uncle Miko's eyes filled with tears as he remembered the harshness of the world, but he thought that if there was so much evil there must be a lot of good as well to compensate for it. Janos's honest, beefy face confirmed him in this conviction. When he arrived in Zugliget, he

walked home from the terminal singing to himself in a low
voice.

'How late you are today,' said Aunt Anna. 'What's new at
the office?'

'Nothing,' replied Uncle Miko with a radiant smile.

GAMES OF THE UNDERWORLD

CHRISTMAS EVE

I T was Christmas Eve, 1944; Budapest was blanketed in thick fog. Few cars were about, the trams had stopped running at noon. Suddenly there appeared a great host of ravens, a cloud of them which flew in from the hills of Buda and settled in the trees of the parks. The air-raids were getting more and more frequent, and as a result the streets were covered in accumulated litter.

The fog lay thickest near the river. Frances Rusko, 52 years old and a widow, an attendant at the Lukacs bathing establishment, lived in a third-floor room-and-kitchen flatlet looking out on to a narrow side-street in the building opposite Police Headquarters on the Pest bank. She had been sick for three days; during that time she had left the house only once because of her gouty foot, to do her Christmas shopping. She was expecting her daughter and her daughter's fiancé for dinner.

She was a big, greying woman with a somewhat protruding stomach, a pair of man's shoes several sizes too large on her feet, red, chapped hands and arms, but her eyes shone with a mocking, youthful gaiety. She had buried three of her children, four remained: two girls who had married and gone off to live in the provinces, one boy at the front, and Evi, the youngest, who was resident teacher in a girls' boarding school. She had stayed alone for a year in the little flat which had been hers for over two decades, and had recently, in a burst of hospitality, taken in a speckled hen, Pinduri.

19

Pinduri was a noisy lodger, but even during the winter she laid an egg every other day.

The old woman laid the table for the dinner party in the room. It was about one o'clock when Evi and her fiancé, also a school teacher, arrived. Laughing and inquisitive, the girl at once ran to the kitchen, dragging the still somewhat awkward, dejected young man after her by the hand.

'It's going to be a wonderful dinner, you'll see, Janos!' she said, and her round laughing face that even weeks of semi-starvation in early winter had not succeeded in marking, shone so sweetly and gently with happiness that it illuminated the whole kitchen. 'It'll be a dinner to remember, you mark my words. What we'll have is mother's secret, of course . . . just look at her, keeping me away from the stove! Let me look, mother,' she begged, 'at least let me peep!'

'Get along with you!' said the old woman, her stomach shaking with laughter.

Evi wrinkled her nose. 'Don't shout at me,' she grumbled. 'How long did you starve yourself to produce this feast, just tell me that!'

'I didn't!'

'A week?' the girl asked severely. 'Two weeks? Three?' She laughed again, with such liquid, warbling turtle-dove laughter that even her fiancé whose brother had been arrested by the secret police that very morning, broke into a smile, and felt easier for a moment.

'She used to starve the whole family for a month,' Evi told her fiancé, beating her two tiny fists together in sudden anger. 'The eight of us lived on soup and mush for a whole month before Christmas till we got so thin that a draught would blow us out through the key-hole, and all the time this old woman here saved every penny in her drawer to put a turkey and twenty four loaves of nut and poppy-seed cake on the table on Christmas Eve . . . What? I'm making it up?' she cried, laughing. 'Just look at her shaking her stomach! By that time we'd all got so weak that we couldn't swallow a single bite—we just stared at the laden table and wept. I suppose that isn't true either? Am I lying? What did you "starve" together for today? Tell me, won't you let me go near the stove to look? And if I die before it's served? You wait, mother, you'll be sorry for upsetting your dearest daughter like this!'

The old woman folded her hands over her stomach and looked at her daughter. 'Nosey!' she said, and her stomach heaved again with laughter. Evi clapped her hand over her lips.

At that moment a piece of plaster, the size of a leaf, detached itself from the ceiling and plopped down on the stove where it crumbled into powder like snow. A crack, the width of a finger, opened in the wall from floor to ceiling. A little kitchen stool standing by the wall jumped straight into the air like a young goat, shaking off the sieve which had lain on it. The thick explosion filled the kitchen like a cloud of dust; for a second none of them could see.

'What was that?' Evi asked. She stood there, very pale, grasping the dresser with both hands.

The old woman fingered her ear. 'I thought I'd gone deaf,' she said.

The kitchen stool jumped again into the air, and a shower of plaster fell from the ceiling. A pot slid slowly along the top of the stove and leapt with a loud clanking noise on to the stone floor of the kitchen. The young girl staggered, and fell against the wall.

'Lucky there was only water in it,' said the old woman, picking up the pot. 'There wasn't an air-raid warning, was there, Janos?'

'There wasn't,' replied the young school teacher, wiping

the blood from his forehead, which had been scratched by a
sharp piece of plaster.

'Are you wounded?' Evi asked. 'What was it?'

The teacher did not answer. Giving the girl a quick look
to make sure she was unhurt, he ran into the room, opened
the window, and looked up at the sky. Evi ran after him.
'Get away from the window, quick!' she cried. 'What are
you looking for?'

The young man turned to face her. The expression on his
face was so extraordinary, such a strange mixture of surprise and happiness that he reminded one of a young mother
gazing at her first-born child.

'It wasn't a plane,' he said quietly.

'What was it then?'

The young man swallowed with emotion. 'It's Christmas
day,' he said.

Evi gazed into his face with rounded eyes.

'Yes,' Janos said, 'the first Russian shell on Christmas day.
Perhaps salvation is at hand. Come!'

He went to the girl and took her in his arms. A third shell
exploded in the wall of a house a little further away; only
the light hanging from the ceiling nodded lazily in recog-
nition.

'Let's go down into the underworld!' the old woman called
from the kitchen. She had already packed their things and
was waiting for them with her coat and scarf on, and a large
jar under her arm. 'I'm taking the lard,' she said, 'lest the
cockroaches eat it up!' Pinduri, the hen, sat on her shoulder,
screwing its head round anxiously.

By the time they had descended the narrow, gaping stairs
into the cellar, the air-raid shelter was already crowded. There
was no electricity, a single oil lamp threw its pale, melancholy
light into the two narrow spaces placed one behind the other
like the two strokes of a T, and were full of chairs, divans

and bare iron bedsteads. The men stood in the lobby round a tub filled with water, wondering what to do, whilst the women exchanged loud excited greetings further in, near the stove set up in the first cellar.

The widow Rusko and her family settled down in the second cellar. 'If we hadn't been struck by lightning,' she grumbled, 'it would have been ready by now.'

Evi winked at her fiancé. 'What would have been ready, mother?' she asked, casually, as if she were not really interested.

The old woman muttered something.

'I didn't hear you,' Evi said. 'What did you say?'

The old woman shrugged her shoulders. 'I said it would be ready by now.'

'What would?'

'Nosey!' said the old woman. 'You'll find out this evening.'

Both started to laugh simultaneously, the old woman pressing her hand to her belly to stop it shaking, and Evi, throwing back her head, laughed so boisterously, so zealously that her round, white throat tensed with the sweet effort, and the entire cellar fell silent and looked at them, smiling for a moment. 'You can't win,' Evi said, 'the old dear's brain is as sharp as a bishop's; I just don't know why, with such gifts, she chose to be a proletarian.'

'Nosey,' the old woman said for the third time that day. 'If I were you, I'd find out why my fiancé is hanging his head.'

Evi glanced quickly at the young man who was gazing ahead silently, deep in thought. 'That's his normal attitude,' she said.

'Perhaps he's hungry,' the old woman suggested.

'When he's hungry he shouts. He's sad like that only when he's happy.'

'Happy?' the old woman broke into gentle mocking laughter.

'Happy as an angel in the wood-cellar,' Evi said.

'If I were intending to marry an insolent chit like you, I'd have joined a funeral society long ago,' said the old woman.

'He's done that,' said Evi, 'but that's not what makes him so melancholy.'

'What then, you school-marm?'

'The fact that he doesn't know what he's getting for dinner,' said the girl, laughing. 'You'll drive us both to our deaths, you'll see, mother!'

The young man indicated by a fleeting smile that he was participating in the conversation with his ears, but he did not raise his head. As the first excitement abated, the talk round them grew quieter; the women rummaged in the food bags, someone was noisily sipping tea from a thermos flask; all eyes turned in that direction. A young girl settled herself under the oil lamp and began to read the Bible.

'So the siege has begun at last!' sighed a voice. Pinduri, the hen, which had been calmly preening itself on the old woman's lap, launched itself with a flap of its wings on to the young school-teacher's shoulder, and knocked on his head with its beak.

'She wants to know why you're so silent,' the young girl said.

'Obviously because he has nothing to say,' said the widow, and, laughing again, dealt the young man a resounding slap on the back.

From time to time a messenger ran up from the cellar into the still deeper darkness of the yard, to inspect the state of the damaged building. Though the gun-fire abated by the evening, and the house had not been hit again, nobody suggested moving back into the exposed flats, so the women began slowly to get the place ready for the night. Pillows, blankets, appeared on the beds and, where there was enough room, armchairs were pushed together and the children bedded down on them. The oil in the lamps burned low, and a candle had to be lit. Evi rose.

'Where are you going?' asked the old woman.

The girl bent down to murmur into her ear. 'We'll go and eat our dinner,' she whispered. 'You stay down here, and we'll bring yours down to you.'

'Go ahead, child,' the widow looked at her, resting her bony old hand with its narrow silver band on the ring-finger, on her daughter's shoulder for an instant. The girl nodded, and ran from the cellar.

It was dark in the flat, and they had to light a candle. Evi closed the windows, put the candle on a chair behind the wardrobe, then, leaning back against the wall, she pulled the young man towards her by the lapels of his jacket.

'Is anything wrong?' she asked him.

'Nothing at all.'

'Sure?'

The young man nodded.

'Has your brother come home?'

'He has.'

'He isn't in trouble?'

'No,' the young man said.

'Sure?'

'Sure.'

Evi gave a sigh of relief. 'I really was badly scared this time. If they'd caught him and found the weapons . . . Thank God it came off!'

'Yes,' said the man.

Evi threw her arms round his neck and kissed him on the lips. Her pale face flushed softly like the sky at dawn, when it feels the approach of the sun. 'Wait,' she whispered. 'The papers are with mother. They're safer with her than with me. Right?'

'Right,' said the young man.

'This is our Christmas,' the girl whispered. 'Let's celebrate it.'

She stirred up the fire in the stove where the big secret, the duck, was waiting, pink and ready, for its initiation, and in a moment the kitchen was filled with its strong, triumphant smell. A bottle of red wine stood on the dresser, and beside it were four loaves of nut and poppy-seed cake as well as a white country loaf rolled up in a tea-towel.

'The old woman certainly has done us proud,' Evi said, in amazement. 'I wonder where she found this beautiful bird.'

She served up the small round duck, which seemed to dance in the hot, voluble, spluttering nut-brown fat round it in the iron roasting-tin.

In places a light foam had collected in round spots on top of the fat which flashed silvery in the candle-light, and in the centre the duck rose, a mound of tenderness and crispness, radiating from under its pink skin. On the right a plate of purple beetroot, on the left, the tart, dream-filled juice of the wine complemented the pink, oily duck. The thick slice of soft white bread near the plates was salvation itself.

'You see,' Evi said, 'this is the short, fat, big-bottomed duck one should always choose because it's the best. Don't ever let me skin it after we're married—it must be roasted in its own fat or it isn't worth eating. You can cut off the fat round its bottom because one doesn't eat it anyway, but the rest . . . ! Now just watch me!' She rolled up her sleeves to the elbow and bent her happy face, bathed in red light, over the pan. 'Look,' she said, 'just see how the skin has slipped up here on the leg, and how nicely the little bone has reddened? I take it between two fingers and make a clean cut

round it, then I lift it a bit . . . it seems to stick a little . . .
did you hear the joint crack? . . . and now it comes off in one
piece as if it had never been there. Now I lift it by its bottom
and stand it on its nose, then I cut into it right and left. At
such times a bit of temper doesn't hurt—it helps you to get
the better of these tough tendons . . . but today I can't be
angry and that's why it's lasting as long as a wet afternoon.
But now you can turn away because I'm going to reach in
with my hand and tear off the breast meat and then I'll
lick my fingers and pick up every little crumb of meat because
that's the best part of it. Don't look! Am I ready yet? No,
not for ages yet! I still have to cut off the wings, scrape the
burnt bits off the side of the pan because that's what tastes
best, and all the time that's going on, you can faint with
hunger. Here's a leg, school-teacher—amuse yourself with
it!'

After dinner, they both fell silent. They just sat gazing at
each other. Once the girl blew out the candle and opened
the window in order to air the room. An over-turned lorry
lay under the window in a tanktrap with two dead soldiers
on the cab. Evi shuddered and closed the window. From the
direction of Buda the guns opened fire again with a dull,
distant rumble.

'We're not going downstairs,' Evi said. 'Come.'

They lay in the bed for the first time since they had met
and fallen in love. When an occasional shell exploded nearby,
the candle fluttered for a moment, turning the room upside
down. Towards midnight, the kitchen door opened, and the
big-framed old woman stopped on the threshold with a candle
held high in her hand. Soundlessly she observed the two
lovers fast asleep in each other's arms, then she nodded,
turned round, and silently closed the door behind her. 'Poor
little things!' she murmured. She squatted down by the stove,
and began to eat the remnants of the dinner. 'They didn't

leave me any wine, the little runts,' she grumbled, and laughed soundlessly, making her stomach wobble. Pinduri, the hen, perched on her shoulder and watched sleepily as the old woman's hand moved up and down in the light of the candle.

DAWN IN DECEMBER

BEFORE flaring up and jerkily stretching forth its squat little flame, bathing the rough wooden shelf and the thin female hand which rested on the wall behind it in a friendly, yellow light, the tall candle had stood silent in the thick darkness, and only a second later did it begin—as if roused to life by its own gleam—to splutter its rapid, early morning sermon. Those who were asleep beneath the cellar's low ceiling woke immediately; and, replying to the greeting of the light with a short, unthinking yawn, a raucous clearing of the throat, or a low moan, the thirty men and women sat up in bed almost simultaneously. Only one stubborn individual snored on undauntedly near the emergency exit. But he too fell silent when a near miss shook the walls and elicited a low tinkle from the small chamber pot which shone with a white gleam under one of the children's beds.

'They're not losing any time today, are they?' said Uncle Lajos, pulling his thick white legs quickly out from under the camel-hair blanket.

'They've certainly got it in for this neighbourhood!' said a younger voice sleepily.

The women remained silent. Someone lit a candle at the back of the cellar, which guttered softly, then suddenly spread an even, smooth carpet of light on to the low-hung ceiling. The crackling of the freshly lit stove could be heard from the next cellar, which was divided from the first only by a batten door. Another shell found its target; again the concrete floor

seemed to shiver, and the crucifix on the wall slid to one side.
The caretaker's four-year-old son sat up in bed, pointed at the
shell-shocked crucifix, and broke into melodious laughter.

'Did they hit us?' asked a lanky, big-boned old maid, who
was sitting bolt upright and motionless on the edge of her
bed, wiping her large bespectacled face from time to time
with a red silk handkerchief.

By now the blasts were shaking the walls almost unceasingly. The vibration spread invisibly under the skin of the
stones, jarring the nerves of the people as they sat dressing
on the edge of their beds, like a long-drawn-out, unanswered
question, slithering back and forth below their consciousness
and seeking vainly for a solution. Only a feeble light came
from the candles burning in the damp close air, so that the
centre of the huge cellar remained plunged in almost total
darkness. It was here, in the darkness, that the tear-stained,
unaired smell of the pillows and blankets collected thickest.

'We can't air the place now,' someone said, looking up, her
head thrown back, at the window under the ceiling which
was covered with a metal plate. A thin iron ladder led up
to it.

'I asked if we'd been hit?' the bespectacled old maid repeated.

'No, that one was a near miss,' replied the retired colonel
next to her, who was so deaf in both ears that he could not
hear male voices at all, and of the female voices only the
shrillest and sharpest were audible to him; despite this, he
enjoyed undivided authority in all things military.

'And that? . . . What was that?' his neighbour, a young
doctor who, for lack of better accommodation, slept on an
operating table covered in white oilcloth, asked, bending close
to the colonel's ear.

'That was another near miss!' answered the optimistic
colonel.

At the back of the cellar, under the candle which was gut-
tering on its shelf, a young girl stood combing her hair;
shadows from her slowly moving arms ran up to the ceiling
with wide, sweeping movements, paused there for a moment,
then—as if reluctant to fall back—sank back into the muddy
darkness below the shelf. Between her lips she held a thin
wire hair-pin. At a new, heavier explosion, the hair-pin fell
from her mouth and dropped, with a tinkle, on to the
floor.

'What are you cooking today? Juliska?' she asked the
caretaker's wife, after bending down to grope for the hair-pin,
cleaning it with her fingers, and sticking it back between her
lips. 'Beans?'

The caretaker's wife shook her head; not beans. 'If I can
go up to the flat this morning,' she said, 'I'll light the stove
and make some cabbage noodles.'

The young girl drew a deep breath, closed her eyes, and
clapped her hand over her mouth. 'Lord!' she exclaimed, 'if
only I could eat an apple-strudel just once more—with lots
of currants and a thick layer of castor sugar on top! . . . That
one hit the house, didn't it?' she whispered, her lips whiten-
ing, and gripping the shelf with both hands. Someone in the
next cellar pushed open the batten door, stopped for a moment
on the threshold, then withdrew, reassured.

'It wasn't this house; perhaps it was the one next door,'
said Uncle Lajos. 'Juliska dear, if you light the stove, I'll give
you a few potatoes and some vinegar to cook for me.'

At the word 'vinegar', the pregnant young woman who
had been gazing silently at her little round belly, a soft,
happy, dreamy smile on her lips, suddenly shut her eyes.
From the white, hissing ball which the word 'vinegar' repre-
sented for her, a sour, acrid smell rose up like a cloud of flies
from a torn carcass, covered the walls and furniture with a
grey sediment, and emitted tiny bubbles that, within seconds,

flew round the cellar, turned red, swelled up and dripped blood all over the floor.

'That was a hit!' the colonel informed his listeners in a booming voice; he had not noticed that someone had fainted behind him, and that the women were busy trying to revive the young woman with toilet water and wet sponges. 'On the other hand it might have been a bomb,' he added thoughtfully, 'one of the small calibre ones . . . 25-50 kilos . . . the kind the Russians use . . .'

When the shelling stopped half an hour later, the cellar emptied; only the children remained—watched over by a few women—and an old couple moved in from one of the neighbouring houses. They opened the air-shaft, and a young girl began to sweep the floor; the rising dust mingled with the cold dawn mists streaming in through the ventilator, and peopled the deserted room with the fresh, familiar images of household chores and cleanliness. It must have been seven o'clock. The old maid pushed her way quickly through the second cellar where the poorer inhabitants of the house had settled, ran along the long, dark corridor opening from it, climbed the winding stairs, and, reaching the yard, looked about her anxiously.

As far as she could make out in the fog, the house was undamaged, and even the door to her flat was unharmed. Her heart always contracted a little as she came up in the mornings, because she never knew whether, instead of her peaceful flat, she was not going to be met by the cornucopia of destruction. But once more she was fortunate: her flat, the only possession she had on earth, had come through unscathed except for a broken window. The old maid set about cleaning the place up; only after she had done that would she wash and have her breakfast. At this time of the morning, before it was fully light, there was always a pause in the shelling, which would last for an hour or two as if, from sheer

humanity and worldy consideration, the besiegers were grant-
ing the inhabitants a small respite to clean themselves after
the ugly, underworld nights.

After shaking the rug, sweeping the ceiling with her
feather duster, and removing the last speck of dust from the
room as it took shape in the slow December dawn, she washed
herself from top to toe, and drank her unsweetened Hungarian tea; then she took the speckled hen which sat under
the sewing machine on her arm, and hurried down the street.
In a few moments she had reached the Stock Exchange from
one of whose destroyed store rooms the blast had swept innumerable dead rats and bats out into the street. She put the
hen down on the sidewalk, tied a long string to its leg, then,
straightening her back, and with a dreamy smile on her broad
face, she began her daily tour of inspection.

The streets were deserted; along Nador Street, in whose
distant reaches could be seen the fog-washed dark mass which
was the Parliament building, in the narrow side streets running down to the Danube, in the bullet-torn walks of Liberty
Square, not a soul was visible, only the fog rolled on above
the wetly shining asphalt. It was cold. Some distance away
smoke came curling out of a cellar window; like some mush-
room growth of underground putrefaction it pushed out into
the street and spread in thick grey bushes over the pavement.

'Perhaps they're baking bread,' said the old maid aloud
with a questioning expression on her face.

The hen was standing still, its feet spread wide, picking
with its pointed beak at the head of a dead rat. Its feathers
shone, its neck was tense; it was the only unmarred creature
among all the ruins. On the opposite pavement lay the body
of a soldier, close by a torn-up tree, its roots stretched towards the sky. A slow cold rain was falling.

The stillness of the street was so absolute that, at a louder
tap of the hen's beak, the old maid was startled, and turned

round to stare suspiciously towards Liberty Square. Behind her, the façade of a tall apartment building caved in, the torn green wallpaper on the rear wall swayed slowly backwards and forwards in the wind. For a while the old maid watched in silence; then she picked the hen up, kissed it, and started out homewards. A reconnaissance plane roared over her head; it was only a matter of minutes before the next raid was due to start.

By the time she reached the hall, the machine guns were crackling, and the anti-aircraft unit on the roof had gone into action. There was a bottle-neck at the head of the cellar steps, and the inhabitants of the house were fleeing, helter-skelter, down them.

'Juliska,' the old maid said to the caretaker's wife, 'tell Uncle Lajos that his soldier son is dead. He is lying on the pavement in front of 28 Nador Street.'

She still had to climb up to the flat, to hide the frightened hen which was nervously jerking its ruffled head at each detonation, in its place under the sewing machine. For a while she pottered round quietly in the flat, then groped her way down to the cellar where the candle had just gone out. Someone lit another.

THE HORSE

IT was dusk. A slow drizzle was falling from the low-lying clouds. Here and there a puddle gleamed amidst the flag-stones of the muddy pavement.

The old man walked quickly in order to get home before dark. From across the street dense, velvety black clouds of smoke thrust their way out of the first-floor windows of a block of flats, accompanied by thin, hissing tongues of flame which bathed the still unbroken panes of the house opposite in a yellow light. The street was deserted—only a dead soldier lay amongst the glass splinters in the middle of the narrow roadway, his face hidden in the crook of his arm.

The old man stopped short in front of a dairy. A brown horse with a lighter-coloured mane stuck its head out into the street from the empty frame of the narrow shop entrance. 'And how did you get in there?' murmured the old man, and bent forward curiously to examine the tiny premises. The horse's rump was pressed against the rear wall of the shop—on which hung an announcement printed on wine-red-paper—and its flanks were caught between the white-painted counter on the right, and an overturned refrigerator on the left.

The old man stepped back a pace, raised his head and read the shop-sign which the blast had blown awry. 'Milk-Butter-Eggs' was the inscription he could make out in the rapidly thickening darkness. He looked at the horse once more, perplexedly, shook his head, and set off homewards again.

The horse pushed the door open with its head, and followed him.

They still had a short way to go. In front walked the old man, his head bowed as he listened thoughtfully to the rhythmical clatter of the horse's hoofs on the wet asphalt behind him. Once, when he turned into a side street, the hoofs fell silent as if the horse had stopped to think; but a moment later the animal broke into an excited trot in which the heart-beats of anxiety were clearly discernible. A little later, to test him, the old man turned down another side street; the horse paused behind him as before, and then followed him again in an alarmed, rapid trot.

'Blind,' the old man muttered moodily, 'blind in both eyes!'

The streets were deserted and silent; there was a faint rattle of machine-gun fire in the distance. Behind the Basilica a woman, bent double, ran with squelching feet across the slushy square and disappeared into a doorway. Further up, the wide street was covered in broken glass; the dark winter sky was fleetingly reflected in it, flashed, and then froze into the glass. It was getting darker every minute.

By the time they reached home, the Russian mine-throwers were heard from the direction of Buda, and a low-flying fighter plane was sweeping over the roof-tops above their heads. But the horse went down the narrow winding cellar steps behind his new master with movements as practised as if he had been assistant porter in a five-storey block of flats for ten years. He stumbled on the last step only, fell on to his knees, and slid on his belly on to the soot-black landing in front of the air-raid shelter. But no sooner had he arrived than he leapt up, his hoofs beating a tattoo, and, bending his head, he galloped into the long corridor which lead to the coal-cellars. Only the yellow sparks rising from his hoofs shone in the Stygian darkness of the night like the punctuation marks of a scream. He neighed long and plaintively, blood streaming from his neck and back; the low ceiling of the cellar had flayed him in three places. As he reached the end of the corridor, he suddenly stopped and hung his head.

Inside the air-raid shelter people were preparing for bed. The unaccustomed noise brought most of the men and some of the women streaming out on to the landing, whence they advanced in single file, peering forward curiously, towards the coal cellar. Here the shelter commander, who was walking at the head of the procession, halted abruptly, and raised his small black kerosene lamp above his head. Wildly gesticulating shadows raced down the two walls and merged at the roots like an evil tangled bush, cowering, motionless, on the ground. Under the dark vaulted ceiling of the cellar the broad illuminated rump of the horse emerged clearly, enclosed in its low-roofed frame.

A woman gave a stifled cry, then men laughed. The squat, grey-moustached janitor clasped his middle in rare good humour. Someone made the sign of the cross. The air raid warden, Audit Office Councillor Pignitzky raised his lamp still higher, and bent forward—as if he were unable to believe his eyes—gazing non-plussed at the animal's thick fair tail.

'Look at the poor thing shaking,' sighed an elderly woman. As if he could understand her, the horse looked back at her, his large brown eyes gleaming in the lamp-light.

'Now you've done it, Uncle Janos,' the air raid warden grumbled.

'What on earth did you bring it here for?'

The old man wiped the sweat from his forehead with the back of his hand. 'If I'd left him outside, he'd have been killed by a grenade,' he said quietly.

No one spoke. People gazed stolidly ahead, their eyes dark-

ening, their teeth cruel and compressed; they looked as if
they were examining the fat, sweating rump of the animal
with the dual passion of pagan guts and Christian love. The
horse looked back at them with an expression of patient con-
ciliation on its face.

'That little lamp gives a good light,' said a skinny woman,
unexpectedly. 'It's got quite bright.'

'Well, he'd have perished outside, that's true enough,'
muttered the janitor thoughtfully.

Aunt Mari, a cobbler's widow, stepped forward and, with
a tiny shy movement drew her wrinkled palm over the
animal's buttocks. The spectacles which she had inherited
from her husband, and which she now wore for piety's sake
only in front of her healthy old eyes—which had no need of
them—flashed with severity in the lamplight.

'Careful, he might kick you !'

'He's old—he couldn't hurt a fly,' said Mr. Andrasi, the
lame waiter. Thus encouraged, the old women drew even
closer to the horse.

'Where did you find him, Uncle Janos?' asked the janitor.

Once again the old man wiped his damp forehead with his
hand, and his sharp, cold eyes slowly examined one by one
the illuminated faces suddenly turned towards him. 'I didn't
find him, he just came,' he said. 'He was standing at the
counter of a cheese store looking out into the street. The
houses opposite were burning, a mine had torn up the road,
and there was a burned-out tank smoking in the middle of
the street. As soon as he heard me he came out of the shop
and followed me. That bit of the street was covered with
corpses—as I was the only living soul, the poor innocent
brute picked on me.'

'Did you speak to him?' asked Aunt Mari.

The man shook his head. 'No, I didn't.'

'How did he get into the shop?' a woman asked.

'How do I know?' the old man replied morosely. 'I don't even know how he got down these stairs considering that he's blind in both eyes!'

'Blind?' Aunt Mari gasped.

For a moment there was silence. Then there was the sound of loud, cheerful children's voices from the direction of the air-raid shelter, and immediately afterwards, like an angry warning from Mount Zion, came the subdued rumble of a distant explosion. The horse's broad rump quivered almost imperceptibly.

'He's frightened!' cried Juli Sovany, the janitress's orphaned niece who lived on her charity, pressing her hand to her heart. 'Good lord, he's terrified!'

A big, heavy-breasted woman standing next to her wiped her eyes. By some strange process of transference, her ageing heart evoked her own blonde childhood from the golden gleam of the horse's tail. In a second, sentimentality touched the women's hearts, their eyes filled with tears, their hair became dishevelled, and their noses reddened; the horse's gentle, nut-brown eye transformed them, metamorphosed Gorgons, into water.

'Well! I'm not going to chase him away,' said the old man slowly. 'Even if the mines spared him, some dirty tramp would certainly slaughter him by the morning.'

Councillor Pignitzky suddenly turned round.

'All right, let him stay,' he said in his slightly cracked voice. 'He'll have to be turned round so that he can stand with his head looking out. Lead him out on to the landing— that's wide enough for him to turn, then back him into the corner and tie him to the door of the coal cellar. Juli, you can clean up after him twice a day—once in the morning and once in the evening.'

'Yes, sir,' said Juli Sovany.

'But what are you going to feed him on?' asked a woman.

'He'd starve to death outside, poor thing,' said Aunt Mari, sighing.

'I'll get him some grass from Liberty Square,' offered the lame waiter, who, even in compassion, tried to serve humanity according to the rules of his trade.

'We'll find something,' people said to each other.

The problem of hospitality thus settled, the procession wandered back to the air-raid shelter. Juli Sovany ran ahead: she still had to warm up the janitor's dinner and make the beds. In her haste, she stumbled over a protruding stone and fell, whimpering quietly, on to her face.

Aunt Mari, the bespectacled widow of the cobbler, trotted at the tail end of the procession beside another widow who worked as laundress for the wealthy families of the nearby Nador Street. The two old women were on friendly terms. They were both short, skinny and tough; when they stood side by side talking it seemed as if two thin candles had burst into tiny flickering flame in the dark and draughty hall of the great big world. What little light they had they spent modestly and wisely on illuminating, not the baffling night, but each other.

'You noticed it too, didn't you, dear?' the laundress asked.

Aunt Mari stopped and turned the severe gleam of the dead man's spectacles on to her friend. 'And what am I supposed to have noticed, Mrs. Daniska?' she asked mildly.

'The light,' the laundress replied, in a whisper.

Aunt Mari nodded silently; she could not even guess what light her friend meant.

'You remember, dear, don't you,' the widow Daniska continued, 'before we started back, Councillor Pignitzky was holding the lamp in his hand. Then he suddenly turned his back on the horse. He held the lamp so low that he completely hid it with his body—and he is a fine figure of a man

—yet the horse did not disappear in the darkness,' the
laundress went on, lowering her voice still more, 'because the
light stayed there, like a halo round its head. I couldn't
believe my eyes—I looked again and again, but there was
such a radiance round it that it seemed as if a star was shining
over its head.'

Aunt Mari did not answer.

'When I stroked it,' she said after a little while, 'it's skin
was as velvety as the petal of a pansy.'

The air-raid shelter consisted of two cellars, connected not
by a door, but by a short, narrow little passage. On the right
of the first cellar a small recess opened, which the most dis-
tinguished denizens, Councillor Pignitzky, the air raid warden, and his family, had appropriated for themselves. The
common people—widowed charwomen, laundresses, day
labourers, an aged barber's assistant, an even more aged porter,
a woman tobacconist, the lame waiter, a retired postman,
navvies, and elderly unemployed, slept in the two wide low-
ceilinged cellars made of quarry stones, on beds and couches
moved down from the flats. The stove, whose flue led out
into the street through the walled-up window of an empty
store-room, stood in the second cellar.

In the first cellar they were playing cards. A wick thrust
into a tin box cast its uncertain, moon-like light from a shelf
over the table. The men sat around the table on kitchen stools;
one of them leant back against the bed and could not stop
sneezing. From time to time the thick shadow of an arm
would race triumphantly up to the ceiling, and then sink
back into obscurity.

'They're not half punishing this neighbourhood today!'
said one of the men, his big red face glowing like the disc
of the sun, bent over his cards. He emitted a long whistle,
and used his broad palm to sweep the bank into his lap.

'Let them!' murmured his neighbour, a young man in

an army blouse. 'They won't get us down here. Who's banker?'

The next player to hold the bank gave a cheerful, energetic sneeze. In answer, two others followed suit, then, like a thick knot at the end of a string, the stout red-faced man finished the scale in his fat, blaring trumpet.

'Card, please,' grunted the soldier.

The walls shook almost continuously under the impact of the Russian heavy artillery. Loud female laughter shrilled from one corner. The sound was as unexpected in the musty, cold cellar, with its damp, greasy walls, as if a chandelier had suddenly been turned on on the ceiling. Juli Sovany was making up a bed in the far corner of the cellar; her angular behind, bent over the bed, rounded out momentarily in the light of that laughter.

In the next cellar the women were busy preparing dinner. Bean soup was boiling in a huge cauldron on the stove, shopping bags, suitcases, wrapped loaves appeared from under the beds; Aunt Mari, the bespectacled widow of the cobbler, placed a small jar of honey beside her on the bed, and waved in excited invitation to Mrs. Daniska, who was squatting on the third bed along from hers, to join her. The cellar lived on shared food, and whenever someone could lay their hands on a delicacy, they shared it dutifully with their closest neighbour. Only two families cooked separately for themselves— the janitor and his wife, and the Pignitzkys, who had their own stove in the recess in which they lived.

'Juli, when you've finished with that bed, bring me a pail of water,' said the pregnant woman.

'With pleasure,' replied Juli.

A squat, pink-faced smiling woman turned to her from the nearby couch. 'I'll bring you the water,' she offered. 'Poor Juli has been on her feet since dawn. What do you need it for?'

The young woman was overcome with confusion. 'I'd like to wash my hair,' she replied in a low voice. 'But I can fetch the water myself, Aunt Rozsi!'

A long, muffled roll like thunder sounded from the direction of the entrance; a bomb must have fallen nearby. A glass slipped from the table and rolled noisily to the wall; flames shot out from the stove. A pale, dark-haired girl began muttering the Lord's Prayer.

'You'll catch a chill, my dear, if you wash your hair in this cold,' the pink-faced woman said, and sneezed. 'I've got one already.'

Sneezes of every pitch sounded from all around as the dust, stirred up by the explosion, irritated the membranes. In the first cellar, a chorus of male noses rang out like machine-gun fire. 'Stop that now, dinner is ready!' cried one of the women. The old, retired postman knelt down on the ground, and pulled a small bottle of plum brandy out of his kit-bag: he threw his head back, and poured a mouthful down past his protruding Adam's apple, then handed the bottle to the lame waiter who was squatting next to him.

'Have one for the fright we had,' he said, 'but go slow, neighbour, there's only a drop left at the bottom!'

'To your good health!' said the waiter, lugubriously.

'Juli, come over here!' shouted someone from the first cellar.

'Yes, sir!' Juli shouted back.

The card-players put down their cards, and turned to the girl as she ran in.

'I hear they've brought a horse into the cellar,' the fat, red-faced man said with a sneeze. 'What sort of a horse is it?'

'A beautiful horse,' Juli replied, folding her hands on her stomach.

'But who brought it?' asked the soldier.

Juli Sovany shook her head vehemently. 'I don't know,' she said, 'I think it came by itself.'

'By itself, by itself!' the fat man frowned with annoyance. 'This isn't a pub that it should just walk in! Can't you talk more intelligently?'

'No,' Juli replied, frightened.

'Is it fat?' someone asked. The girl nodded. The soldier clicked his tongue. 'Bring it in here!' he shouted at the girl. Juli promptly turned round and began to run towards the door, half-way there she stopped and, pressing her back to the wall, turned round slowly.

'It can't be brought in,' she said excitedly, 'It's blind!'

'Then lead it, idiot!' the soldier bawled at her.

'I can't,' Juli shook her head. 'It's back is bleeding.'

By now everybody was laughing.

'No one told you to sit on its back, stupid,' said the fat man, getting up.

He stretched, and tapped the girl playfully on the head. 'Don't forget to clean my boots before morning, do you hear?'

'Yes, sir,' said Juli, and ran back into the second cellar. The men followed her more slowly. As they passed the recess, a greasy smell of pancakes assailed their noses from the direction of the Pignitzky's stove; the fat tailor, who was walking ahead, turned back and winked at his companions—it was as if the whole expanse of his big face winked.

'What are you having for dinner, Counsellor?' he called into the recess.

'Only some leftovers from midday, Mr. Kovacs,' the woman's voice replied. 'I've used up the last of my flour to-day.'

'Dear me, dear me!' Mr. Kovacs wagged his head. 'The last of your flour!'

The men grinned at each other, walked in single file up to the stove, and sat down on their beds, each with a plate of bean-soup. At such times it was forbidden to sneeze, because if someone did, the soup spilled from the plates on to

one's own or one's neighbour's trousers; as a result, sniffing,
flaring and violently grimacing nostrils bent over the plates.
They were still at dinner when the news came—no doubt
brought by the janitor who had peeped out into the street
for a second—that Anglo-American heavy bombers must
have been over the town because the third and fourth floors
of the house opposite had completely caved in; the rubble was
standing man-high in the street.

The night threatened to be stormy, and the besieging army
appeared to be preparing for an attack. The men standing
round on the landing moodily inhaled the smoke of their
cigarettes, and the more timid soon retreated to safer shelter.
The dull thud of the missiles came rolling down the spiral
staircase of the cellar in endless succession, like evil black
pearls. The anti-aircraft gun installed on the roof of the next
building coughed uninterruptedly, and when, at times, there
was a brief pause between two rounds, one could immediately
distinguish the unearthly, brutal humming of the fighters
circling over the house and the wild teeth-gnashing of their
machine-guns. When a bomb exploded close by, the old
porter who was smoking his pipe near the stairs was sick,
brought up his dinner and then retired into the shelter to
go to bed.

Inside, people were gradually falling silent in the wincing
light of their oil-lamps, and were beginning to accustom
themselves to the approaching night. The young pregnant
woman drew her foot-stool close to the stove, and, bending
down, quickly soaped her hair; a woman standing beside her
poured fresh warm water over the long gleaming soapy hair,
while another warmed two towels in the oven so that the
young woman should not catch cold. Juli Sovany was squatting by the next bed unlacing the old tobacconist's shoes.
Aunt Mari retired to a corner under the light of the candle;
thanks to her youthful and unimpaired eyesight, she was

able to repair Mrs. Daniska's pitifully ragged petticoat before going to bed. The pale, dark-haired girl fell asleep with the Bible in her hand; her neighbour, one of the charwomen, was already snoring gently. In the first cellar, however, they were still pushing furniture around. The old porter whose bed stood under the ventilator changed places with the young soldier: he could no longer face sleeping beneath the air-shaft since the explosion, which had upset his sensitive stomach. It was not a bad bargain because his new neighbour, the waiter, although he bleated in his sleep like a herd of mountain goats pursued by wolves, was still offering his lucky right and left-hand neighbours a little bacon at break-fast time.

Inter-bed conversation died down, the older people slipped slowly into the night. Even the explosions seemed to have become less frequent, and at times complete silence reigned in the cellar for a whole minute. In one of the longer pauses, however, an unexpected sound penetrated the cellar from the direction of the landing: the horse outside broke into a loud, sharp neigh.

Aunt Mari raised her head, and put her hand behind her ear.

'Good Lord, he must be hungry!' cried the pregnant young woman, sitting up in bed with a jump—owing to her condition, she was allowed to occupy the bed alone.

Juli Sovany, who was cleaning the janitor's boots, clapped her hand to her mouth with a frightened gesture: some of the shoe-cream settled on her nose, which began to shine brightly. The widow Daniska crossed herself; Mr. Kovacs sneezed.

'He must be standing right outside the door asking to be let in,' said the janitor.

The whole cellar listened with bated breath; after a few seconds of silence the lonely, gentle neighing was heard again.

'He wants his dinner!' Juli cried, and, in her surprise, dropped the janitor's boot. The pregnant woman jumped out of bed in her bare feet; Mrs. Daniska also scrambled out from under her red and white checked eiderdown, and in a moment the whole cellar was up. His lips shiny, and his forehead puckered with annoyance, Councillor Pignitzky, the air raid warden, emerged from his recess like a weather-cock.

'What's all the fuss about?' he demanded irritably. 'Has the building collapsed?'

'The horse wants to come in, Councillor!' explained Aunt Mari excitedly.

'He probably wants to go to bed,' the air raid warden grumbled. 'I knew there'd be trouble. Where are you going?'

'We must feed the poor thing,' the old laundress said. 'God knows when he last had a meal.'

Pignitzky waved his hand; the thick shadow of his arm ran up the murky cellar wall as threateningly as Cain's fractricidal cudgel. A second later an ear-splitting explosion shook the red brick floor.

'He'll have to be slaughtered,' said the Councillor when he regained the hearing of his temporarily deafened ear, and the spasm contracting his heart had eased. 'We can't keep him here anyway.'

'God forbid!' Aunt Mari cried threateningly. 'We won't hear of it!' said the pregnant young woman, covering her eyes with her hands as if in self-defence. An old charwoman suddenly broke into loud sobs. In the meantime the men, too, had got out of bed, and the lame waiter, his face flushed, shook his stick menacingly at the shelter commander. 'Not on your life!' he screeched in a thin voice overflowing with fury. 'You won't stick your knife into an innocent animal that came here to seek shelter! We'll have something to say about that!'

The old porter, who was still smarting from the memory

of his regurgitated dinner, nodded approvingly. 'It would be
a pity to kill such a valuable animal!' said the retired postman, starting out behind Mrs. Daniska's back towards the
double wooden door of the cellar.

The horse was indeed in the lobby, but not alone. Beside
him stood Uncle Janos, washing his wounds with a pail of
luke-warm water in the light of the hurricane lamp which
swung on a nail in the wall. The horse stood motionless, his
head held proudly, looking with his gentle brown eyes
straight into the eyes of the crowd that pressed through the
door, stopped, startled, and then retreated a step.

'I bet he isn't blind,' Aunt Mari said to herself while her
reluctant nostrils took small sniffs of the raw smell of the
humid, steaming animal hide.

'We should like to feed him,' Mrs. Daniska announced in
a loud voice.

The man did not answer; he was examining the horse's
back. Only now did it become apparent how thoroughly he
had rubbed down the horse.

'Don't you think he should be fed, Uncle Janos?' Mrs.
Daniska asked shyly.

'You took your time,' grumbled the man. 'What have you
brought?'

The animal's skin shone so youthfully and beautifully in
the shaft of light cast by the hurricane lamp that Aunt Mari
involuntarily closed her eyes.

'I brought him a slice of bread,' she announced.

'Me too,' said the retired postman.

'I brought a lump of sugar.'

There was a silence. People looked at each other.

'That's a great help!' growled Uncle Janos.

A horse will eat neither bean soup nor bacon; nor honey
either. The grey-moustached, tubercular barber's assistant
offered the contents of one of his two straw mattresses; he

was city-bred, and thus could not know that a horse will use straw only to lie on, not to eat.

'Has nobody a little maize?' asked the lad in the army blouse.

'I've got half a sackful,' said one of the laundresses. 'My son brought it from Torokbalint, but I couldn't find a goose to feed it to. It's upstairs.'

By ten o'clock most of the Russian long-range guns had fallen silent; a calm, starlit night descended on the town. As the old laundress still did not have the courage to go upstairs, Uncle Janos climbed up himself.

He went up the back-stairs as that side of the building was more protected from the mines; when he reached the open corridor, he started to run, and ran all the way to the old woman's flat. However, he could not find the sack of maize under the bed despite his search; all he could find were a few stripped cobs in the corner of the larder.

The room had one opening on to a narrow side street of the Danube quay. If one leaned out, one could see the moonlit river and, across on the other bank, the dark Castle Hill crowded with cupolas. The cold, whistling wind ruffled the surface of the river into tiny, silvery waves, and its sudden gusts ruffled the torn, gold-flowered wall paper. Like an arrow shot forth by the hill itself, the Church of St. Matthew strove darkly towards the moonlit sky; the houses beneath, in which all human consciousness had become extinct since the beginning of the siege, gazed at the deserted river with their dead eyes. The town grew and ran riot in the moonlight like an undisciplined monster from whose stammering only one sound emerged clearly: the rattle of a distant machine-gun. From behind the Parliament building the river swept along in its reflection the red glow of a burning house, in the direction of the Chain Bridge.

The old man shivered, and retreated from the window. For

a while he stood there scratching his head and staring out
into the night without moving.

He was overcome by the kind of tiredness one feels when
one is trying to solve a riddle to which there is no solution.
He looked round the dark room, then went up to the wall
and, with an irritable movement, tore off a fluttering piece of
wallpaper.

As he was leaving the flat, he met the old laundress at the
door. 'I was frightened something had happened to you,' said
the latter, panting. 'I couldn't think why you stayed away so
long unless you got hurt on the way. That's why I came up
—though I was so scared that I fell down on the second
floor.'

Fresh shots were heard from the direction of the Danube,
and then came the jerky rattle of a machine-gun.

'What's that?' asked the laundress, startled. 'Are the
Russians as close as that?'

The old man shrugged his shoulders. 'Of course not,' he
replied moodily. 'They're machine-gunning the Jews on the
river bank.'

'Dear Lord, what a world we live in!' the old woman
sighed.

The first bombers appeared over the Pest side early the next
morning. Flying low over the roof-tops, they machine-gunned
the anti-aircraft gun installed on top of the neighbouring
house, and now and again a bomb fell on the deserted houses
like a coarse oath spat out by the cold winter dawn. At ten
o'clock it was still impossible to get out to the yard for water.

In the stuffy cellar people lay listless, motionless and
hungry in their beds. Sometimes a group would go out on to
the landing to smoke a cigarette, but after fifteen minutes
they would return, their fingers stiff with cold, to the stove.
In the corridor Mr. Kovacs was sawing up an uprooted tree
which he and two others had dragged in on the janitor's

sleigh on one of the calmer nights from Liberty Square; as they had to economise on both light and fuel, most of the cellar-dwellers assembled in the second cellar round the stove and a single oil lamp. The lad in the army blouse opened a free cobbler's shop in one corner, and, so far as his skill allowed, repaired the damaged shoes of the inhabitants one after the other. The retired postman sat patching his torn shirt, looking down at it through his steel-rimmed spectacled eyes; Aunt Mari thought of her husband with many a sigh.

From time to time one of the old women would go out to the coal cellars to see whether the horse was still there. The animal stood, hanging its head in the pitch-dark corridor, and refused to lift it even when someone stroked his neck. His smooth damp skin twitched as if he were shaking off a fly. Once, in the course of the morning, he neighed plaintively, but that was the only sign of life he gave.

It was midday before Uncle Janos and the lame waiter were able to start out for Liberty Square. They took a coal-sack along with them; instead of a sickle, they had a long bread knife. The bombers had vacated the low, leaden, dripping sky, and for the time being the Russians were shelling the town from the direction of Buda only, so one could walk with relative safety on one side of the street. Here and there, bomb craters loomed darkly in the caved-in walls, splintered glass and rubble; in one place a burst water-main had flooded the street ankle-deep; a big china doll, its arms flung wide, floated on the dark, seething water. There were hardly any people about; an occasional soldier hurried past with lowered head, and sometimes a stray dog would scuttle into the ruins baring its teeth.

They had not reached Liberty Square when Juli Sovany overtook the two men. They were just skirting a tank-trap, in the depths of which lay an overturned German lorry and two dead soldiers with their faces in the mud beside it.

'What the hell are you following us for?' demanded the waiter.

The girl shrugged.

'Speak up, girl. Why did you come?' Uncle Janos urged her.

'I just came to help you,' said Juli, 'so that we get it done sooner.'

'We don't need you. Go on home!' the waiter ordered. Juli did not answer, but bent her head and tramped silently on beside them. Her thin body, huddled in a big black shawl, huge cracked men's shoes on her feet, swayed to and fro in the icy wind like something in a fairy tale. The clouds, swollen with snow, sank so low that the street went utterly dark; one could hardly see more than ten steps ahead in the thick fog which rolled up from the river.

'The Councillor wants to slaughter him!' the girl announced after a while. A second later she stumbled and would have fallen on her face had not Uncle Janos caught her arm.

'I've fixed that!' said the waiter in a superior tone of voice.

Juli shook her head violently. 'You haven't fixed it,' she replied nervously. 'He said it again just after you'd gone. He said there was nothing to feed him with anyway, and he'd only starve to death.'

The waiter stopped in his tracks. 'That's none of his business,' he grumbled. 'Since when has he worried about some-one else's food?'

In the meantime they had reached Liberty Square, where they went diligently to work. Cutting grass with the short-handled bread knife and the kitchen knife Juli had brought with her was a pretty clumsy business. Fortunately the lawn had not been mown since the autumn, so the grass was long enough, but the infantry and artillery crossing the square had trampled the wet, rusty grass-blades into the soil so that it was difficult to find a healthy, upstanding patch. The girl knelt down on the ground, and the two men followed her example. Their fingers soon grew stiff from the wet grass and the frozen clods. The guns from Buda opened up only intermittently, but one of the shells landed in the National Bank building behind them, and left a ragged smoking hole in the wall.

Juli straightened up and stared at the house. 'I hit him,' she said suddenly. 'I hit him,' Juli repeated, and her eyes filled with tears.

'Whom?'

'Councillor Pignitzky,' the girl whispered.

The waiter stared at her as if he feared she had taken leave of her senses.

'Aunt Mari was so furious that she shouted at him,' Juli continued, wiping a glistening tear from her protruding cheekbone with her fist. 'And the other women started wailing, then Aunt Daniska pulled the Councillor's sleeve and screeched so loudly that I got nervous and hit Mr. Pignitzky. But it didn't hurt him because he didn't even turn round.'

Uncle Janos stopped cutting grass, straightened up, and gave the girl a long, searching look from his small eyes. The lame waiter laughed so hard that he almost fell over.

'What is there to laugh at?' the girl asked, offended. 'I know that we are born to do our duty, not to be happy. Still, that horse wasn't born to be slaughtered.'

'And what about people?' asked Uncle Janos.

The fog had grown so dense that they tended to move away from each other without noticing it. It seemed to wrap them from head to foot in a thick grey layer of cotton-wool. It was getting late, dusk merged with the earthly gloom, and it seemed advisable to return home. Uncle Janos lifted the half-filled sack on to his shoulder, and Juli took the lame waiter's arm to help him over the frozen slippery mounds of earth.

On the corner of Nador Street, they came to a sudden halt.

Steps sounded from behind the curtain of fog, soft, squelching steps, as if a long, invisible procession were approaching through the sticky mud. First to emerge from the fog was the figure of a policeman, and behind him, in fours, came blurred swaying shapes with huge bundles on their bent backs or over stuffed sacks under their arms; one old woman was completely doubled up under the weight of a gigantic black travelling bag, which stretched her emaciated arm to breaking point—a man was staggering along pushing a pram, and two people, like rather denser portions of fog, carried bulky grey eiderdowns on their shoulders. As far as one could make out in the dim light, the procession consisted mainly of elderly men and women and small children who also carried bundles on their backs, and were walking with terror-stricken faces among the adults. Uniformed men with Arrow-crosses on their armbands marched on both sides of the procession, their rifles covering it.

Juli Sovany pinched the waiter's arm in fright. 'What's going on, Mr. Andrasi?' she whispered in the man's ear.

'What are you pinching me for?' the waiter cried irritably. 'Can't you see it's the Jews?'

'Jews!' the girl repeated, horrified. 'Where are they taking them?'

Receiving no answer, she drew her arm from under the waiter's, and clutched Uncle Janos's arm with both hands. 'Where are they taking them?' she whispered, raising herself on tiptoe to reach the old man's ear.

'How the hell should I know?' he snapped. 'Stop pulling my arm, do you hear?'

In places, the billowing fog penetrated so deeply between the columns that it would suddenly isolate an entire section of the procession. A grey-haired woman dragged herself past them, her hump bigger than her back; the wind blew her long hair steeply up into a halo of weakness. A long thin arm holding a stick, the end of which disappeared into the swirling vapour, reached out from another moving recess of the fog. Here and there a lonely head would rise above it, further on a leg would sink into the billows which immediately swallowed it up together with the invisible trunk following it. When the smoky veil thinned out for a moment, one could glimpse the blazing house on the other side of the street, its flickering flames colouring the procession that wound its way below it a bright, burning red. The roof-beams crackled, pistol shots were heard from the end of the line.

A tall, skinny woman stumbled past them, dragging a little boy along behind her.

'Save my son!' she whispered hoarsely, turning her bloodless face towards Uncle Janos. The man turned away immediately.

'Look out!' he shouted to Juli, who had stepped forward. He pulled her back. 'If they catch you they make you join the line!'

For a moment the fog round the tall woman dispersed, and her face, as it stared back at them, was as sharply outlined against the glare of the flames as a question at the confessional. Juli looked up to the sky. Clear before her eyes was the Angel of Death hovering in the rain of sparks above the woman's head. The shadow of the huge sword in its hand was falling across the woman's face.

Suddenly Juli let go of Uncle Janos's arm; holding her skirt down to her side with both hands, she ran up to the Arrowcross man who was walking at the head of the procession.

'Where are you taking them, sir?' she asked, in her clear, courageous voice. In the burning house, a beam crashed to the ground with an explosive thud, and was dully submerged in the soft sea of fog.

'Go to hell, or you'll find out for yourself!' the Arrowcross man growled.

Juli joined her hands entreatingly. 'Please let them go, sir!'
she begged, raising her tear-stained little face to the uniformed
man. The latter walked on in silence, his head bowed. The
burning house was left behind, but Juli did not mind; she
stumbled on with hurried little steps behind the Arrow-cross
man, and at times when she reached his side, raised her
clasped hands to him in a gesture of supplication. Then someone took her by the scruff of her neck, spun her round, and
planted a heavy boot so hard on her behind that she fell face
downwards in the mud.

By the time she got home to the air-raid shelter, the women
were already busy preparing the evening meal. The card-
players' table shone in a fairy-like light; as the cellar had
deprived them of the common night-light, Mr. Kovac's had
offered them a huge, twisted pink candle from his own store
for the evening ceremony. Involuntarily Juli stopped by the
table and, bending forward, sniffed the long pink stem and
the golden petals vibrating above it; they had a devout,
Christmas eve-like scent. For a while she smelt it dreamily,
then wiped her nose with the back of her hand; then she ran
into the second cellar, retreated into a corner and squatted
down on a foot-stool.

The women were gay; here and there loud laughter rang
out below the high ceiling. Because of the fog the guns had
been silent almost since noon, and planes did not come over;
so those in the mood could take a walk in the yard in the
fresh air, or go up to clean the flat, wash and do a bit of
laundry; one of the women even took time to bake a small
white loaf from the last of her flour. They returned to the
shelter with their hearts more at ease; perhaps, they thought,
they would survive the siege after all.

'They say the Russians have been driven back in Buda,'
related the janitor's wife who had even received a visitor that
afternoon.

'I wonder . . .' the old porter wagged his head.

'But on this side they're advancing into Rakosszentmihaly,' said another woman who had paid a neighbourly visit to the next air-raid shelter in the afternoon. 'I talked to the soldier son of the Sabos family a while back; he's in the signal corps, you know.'

'I wish it was all over,' sighed Aunt Mari.

The women did not dare imagine how it would end. The two-fold wisdom of age and poverty did not inquire into details: they made do with the featherweight, wonderful hope that they might stay alive and go on cleaning the rich families' homes and laundering their dirty clothes. The most demanding of them was the widow Daniska; she would have liked to see her daughter once more before she died, but her daughter had married someone in Transylvania, and heaven alone knew whether she was still alive.

'It's easy for you, dear,' she would say to Aunt Mari, 'you have no one in the world to mourn if they were to perish!'

'Not even you, Mrs. Daniska?' Aunt Mari would ask, breaking into gentle laughter with the whole of her wrinkled old face.

The thick fog penetrated the lobby of the cellar from the courtyard; when they opened the door, a white rag of mist would slide into the cellar and draw into the air the shapes of the dangerous night. But inside the accustomed landscape had become so intimately warm, familiar and safe that even the janitor's little boy, who was always whining, calmed down, and the other children virtually unsettled the whole cellar with their happy shouts and explosive giggles.

'Have you seen Juli?' the janitor's wife asked. 'Where has that girl gone to now?'

'She ran out of the house at noon,' someone said, 'but I haven't seen her since.'

'She may have slipped out to follow Uncle Janos to Liberty

Square,' a woman said. 'Though he's been back for a long while.'

'I hope nothing's happened to her!'

'A bad penny always turns up,' said the janitor's wife, and sneezed.

Juli squatted motionless in the dark corner, making herself as small as possible, and listening zealously to the conversation. The retired postman's high, piled-up bed behind which she had sheltered hid her completely. But before evening fell they found her. It was Aunt Mari who discovered her with a severe flash of her inherited spectacles.

'So you've been sitting here all the time,' she said, lowering her voice involuntarily so as not to betray the girl. 'Were you asleep, you poor little thing? Come now, help me fetch some water.'

For a moment Juli did not answer, then she said loudly, 'No!'

'Help me fetch some water!' repeated Aunt Mari more loudly.

'I won't help!' said Juli again, throwing back her head.

For a while Aunt Mari looked at her thoughtfully, then she shrugged and turned away. The cellar calmed down. When even the lame waiter had stopped sneezing and they had put out the night-light, Juli slipped on tip-toe from the cellar, pulled the double wooden door carefully shut and, still on tip-toe, started out towards the coal-cellar. It was pitch-dark in the corridor, but the horse's warm smell guided her.

'Sh-h!' she said when, sensing her approach, the animal snorted nervously. She laid the palms of her hands on the horse's velvet-soft nose. 'Be quiet!' she begged him, and gave his neck a reassuring pat. Then, squatting down on the thin layer of straw at the horse's feet, and leaning her back against the wall she pulled the big black shawl closer to her breast. Dawn was breaking, an ashen grey light was creeping up the wall from the ventilator which opened on to the courtyard, when Councillor Pignitzky, on his way to the lavatory, turned into the corridor. Juli ran silently up to him, and stabbed him to the heart with the bread-knife she had brought back with her from Liberty Square.

Outside it was already much lighter. She roamed the streets all day, taking refuge in the nearest doorways against the infrequent raids, then stayed for a while with an old cook who had known her mother in her girlhood.

She was sitting on a pink cloud floating high up in the sky—this was what she dreamed as she sat on the narrow wooden bunk under the pink blanket—and the horse was standing beside her, holding its head up proudly, and happily shooing away the heavenly pink flies with its tail. The cloud swam away over Budapest, crossed the silvery Danube and hung suspended for a while over Mount Gellert. Wherever it passed, it was accompanied on earth, not by a shadow, but by a brilliant pink light which illuminated the streets and the steep roofs. Juli leaned comfortably back against the soft cumulus and folded her hands across her stomach. They were flying so high that her gaze could encompass half the country.

'Thank you for saving my life,' said the horse. Its neck shone with a pink glow in the cloud's strong light.

Juli swung her legs above Mount Gellert. 'I did what I could,' she replied modestly, 'otherwise they would have made you join the procession too, wouldn't they?'

'Certainly,' said the horse.

The cloud started off again, but this time it flew towards Kobanya. By the time Juli returned to the wooden bunk, morning had come. She threw the shawl over her head and ran up the staircase. At the front door a soldier stopped her.

'Where are you running to, Miss?' he asked.

'To my mother,' said Juli quickly, then she ran through

the door, and flew, like an arrow, along the early morning street. At the first corner she stopped for a moment, turned her little snub nose, reddened with weeping, back in the direction whence she had come, then slipped into a side street. She was never seen again.

THE PARCEL

IN the morning, when they opened the double door of the air-raid shelter, the draught which swept in from the direction of the yard stirred all the occupants of the cellar to an excitement like an exclamation. The bottles on the shelves clicked together, the blankets on the beds fluttered, dust rose up from the floor.

'Shut that door!' growled a man's voice. In the bed opposite the door, a girl stuck her tousled head up from her pillow, and blinked in amazement as she regarded the cloud of dust churning the air at the foot of the bed. To right and left people sat up abruptly or propped themselves up on their elbows.

'What's happening?' someone cried. Aunt Mari, the cobbler's widow, lit a candle and raised her arm, thus softly illuminating the face of the old woman next to her.

'Are you alive, Mrs. Daniska?' she asked.

'Why shouldn't I be alive?' the other mumbled indifferently. 'What did you wake me up for?'

'Did I wake you?' Aunt Mari asked, amazed. 'Didn't you hear the house cave in over our heads?'

'Well, what can I do about it?' grumbled the widow Daniska. 'Do you expect me to stick it together again?'

The shelling seemed to have stopped; not a sound came from the yard. There was not even a crack on the low ceiling of the cellar, and the darkly sweating walls were unscathed. The herald of the event, the tall cloud of dust, crumbled suddenly and collapsed on the floor as if, on reaching its goal, it

were disclaiming its own existence. People got out of bed and
began to dress with quick, silent movements.

By the time Uncle Janos, the deputy air-raid warden, had
pulled on his boots and put his Transylvanian fur-cap on his
head, his neighbour, Mr. Andrasi, the lame waiter, who
always slept fully clothed and wearing his hat, had already
returned from his reconnaissance. The yard side of the building had received a direct hit on the first floor, he announced;
however, the damage was not serious, the shell had only
knocked a small hole in the wall, and blown a piece out of
the landing.

'But even that isn't too bad,' he said, 'because it hasn't
torn off the whole of the landing, but only broken a piece
out of it. So our nice little landing is now hanging from the
house wall like skin from a sausage.'

'How am I going to get into my flat, then?' asked the old
seamstress.

The waiter shrugged his shoulders.

'What do you want to get in there for?' he grumbled.
'Do you want to clean up again? Time enough for that when
peace comes.'

The women lit the stove, fetched water, made the beds,
swept the floor; the men went out on to the landing to smoke,
or climbed up to the yard to look at the broken landing with
appraising glances. The young man in the army blouse ran
over to the baker's shop to see whether it was open. Half an
hour later, as he was returning empty-handed, he ran into
Aunt Mari on the stairway. The old woman flashed him a
disapproving look through the spectacles she had inherited
from her late husband.

'Why are you roaming the streets, child?' she asked re-
proachfully. 'The Arrow Cross men will catch you!'

'And why are you climbing up to the third floor?' replied
the lad. 'Do you want to catch birds?'

As he reached the dark, narrow, winding staircase which led down to the cellar, he picked the frightened old woman up in his arms, and, laughing loudly, ran down the steps with her.

'This way we get down quicker—true, Aunty?' he said, setting the small body carefully down on the floor next to the wall. 'Coffee must be ready, I think—I can smell it.'

Aunt Mari shook her head. 'Oh dear,' she said, 'I can't eat now—I've seen a dead body.'

'Where?'

'Right under my window!' the old woman sighed.

The lad stared at her. 'Where?' he repeated. 'Are you sure it was under your window? On our pavement?'

'You can look right down into the poor soul's face from my window,' explained Aunt Mari.

The soldier emitted a long whistle. 'That's bad,' he said, 'if he really is on the pavement.'

After breakfast, the men filed out on to the landing to discuss the day's joyless events. The Russian bombers droned harshly over the roof-tops, their machine-guns biting and chopping into the bare walls of the houses; the anti-aircraft gun on the roof of the neighbouring bank coughed unceasingly. When the fire died down for a moment they could hear from the yard above the slow, monotonous trickle of the thawing snow—a gentle reminder of the winter.

'It's a fact that he's lying on our pavement,' the soldier reported, 'right under Aunt Mari's window.'

'A civilian?'

'A civilian.'

Uncle Janos, deputy air-raid warden, sucked the ends of his walrus moustache into the corners of his mouth and remained morosely silent. 'Well, if he really is a civilian, and is lying on our pavement, then we'll have to bury him,'

sighed the squat, pink-faced, white-haired janitor. He looked
worried. 'And, what's more, we'll have to ask some of the
women to help—we can't manage on our own!'

The day before there had appeared a decree from the Mayor,
according to which the tenants of each block were given 24
hours to bury any dead civilian found lying outside it, in
the nearest public park. The nearest public park was Szabad-
sag Square, but heavy German tanks had moved in, and the
Germans would not let anyone go close.

'Jozsef Square is full,' said the retired postman. 'We'll have
to take him to Erzsebet Square.'

How were they to carry the corpse to Erzsebet Square,
which was a good twenty minutes away, and in the line of
fire of the Russian mortars? How were they to bury him
when they could only muster two shovels between them, not
a single pick-axe, and the ground was frozen hard? What
were they to cover him with when the people in the cellar
were so poor that one was lucky if one had a winding sheet
for oneself?

By evening, however, man's cunning had solved even these
painful questions. After dark, at the hour of the daily card-
battle, while the women, grouped round the stove, the evening light of the embers illuminating their faces, smoothed
from their minds the wrinkles which had accumulated there
during the day, the men stole out one by one from the
shelter, and, led by Uncle Janos, marched along the front of
the block. They walked in single file, close to the wall so as
not to be seen, under Aunt Mari's window. The dead man
lay close to the kerb, his body straight, his black double-
breasted winter coat moulded to his body as if he had carefully arranged it beneath him before lying down; only his
hat had rolled from his head, and his long grey hair hung
down in disorder on the snow-caked paving stones. The moon
shone straight into his face: his eyes were open.

The old men stood round him. The waiter took off his hat, then, sneezing violently, stuck it quickly back on his head. 'Let's hurry,' someone said. Although not a soul was in sight in the narrow, moonlit street, the pure, beautiful night could easily have enticed a bored cellar-dweller out into the street, or a Russian plane above it.

'Take his feet,' Uncle Janos instructed Mr. Kovacs, the fat tailor whose flaming red face hovered like a lamp over the snow. 'And you, Mr. Andrasi, help him. The rest of us will take his shoulders. Ready?'

The next corner of the block was not too far away, but the old men broke out into a sweat. The dead man was heavier than they had thought. The retired postman wiped his forehead with a red and white checked handkerchief. They put the body down so quickly that its head hit the pavement with a thud.

'Sh-h!' said the old postman, looking round nervously.

The lame waiter stepped back and took a careful look at the body. 'Is it lying all right?' he asked. 'Shouldn't we put it nearer the wall?'

'He was lying on the edge of the pavement at our place,' said the soldier. 'That's his natural position.'

The lame waiter knelt down on the pavement and smoothed down the dead man's overcoat on both sides of his body. 'Lift him up a bit in the middle, will you?' he grumbled. 'I can't do it alone. You're right—let him lie the way he was.'

It was a mild night; melting snow dripped from the roof-tops. Some fell on to the dead man's face.

'Shouldn't we move him a bit?' said the retired postman, crossing himself involuntarily.

'What for?'

The old man did not answer. The lad in the army blouse burst out laughing. 'It will be quite a surprise,' he said, and

his white teeth flashed in the moonlight, 'when they wake up
in the morning and find a body to bury. God, won't that be
an upheaval?'

'And they won't have to take too long about it, either,'
muttered Uncle Janos.

'Why not?' The waiter scrambled to his feet. 'I get it,' he
said. 'The weather has been very mild since yesterday.'

'Lord, what a surprise!' repeated the soldier, pushing his
cap to the back of his head expansively. 'How these gentlemen will complain when they have to drag it all the way to
Erzsebet Square . . . What's the name of that pig-faced councillor who lives on the first floor here?'

At that, even the old porter could not help laughing.
'And Director Lorincz,' he whispered, poking a moonlit finger
towards the flashing windows of the house, 'and Mr. Finiasz,
the lawyer . . . and Bor, the solicitor on the third floor, the
one who used to make me take a parcel for him every
week . . .'

'And now you're sending him one,' said the retired postman.

Suddenly a cold wind rose from the Danube. A broken
window on an upper floor flew open, and its cracked panes
swept the pavement with their silvery reflection. A single
shot was heard in the distance.

The tailor turned back. 'They're coming,' he growled, 'be
careful!'

There was a sound of light splashing behind them, as if
the small puddles hiding in the dark had suddenly begun to
talk. Two small, but denser, shadows detached themselves
from the shadow at the foot of the wall which cut obliquely
across the street, and, emerging into the moonlit part of the
pavement, came two more shadows.

'Aunt Mari and old Mrs. Daniska,' muttered the air-raid
warden. 'What ill wind blew these two here?'

The two old women teetered towards them holding tightly on to each other. 'Have you moved my dead man?' Aunt Mari shouted from some distance away. 'You see, they did move him—didn't I tell you so, Mrs. Daniska?'

'They moved him in front of the next house,' the old laundress stammered, crossing herself.

Aunt Mari flashed her spectacles. 'They were quite right to do so, Mrs. Daniska,' she answered. 'We'll have plenty to do, burying our own dead.'

'Why are there so many old women?' said the lame waiter under his breath.

Aunt Mari bent over the dead man. 'And this one isn't a boy any longer, either,' she said. 'Why didn't someone close his eyes?'

'Because it was impossible,' the waiter growled. 'I tried, but it was too late.'

The dead man looked up at the sky through wide-open eyes as if he were watching the moonlight. Aunt Mari bent down lower, touched the woolly black wintercoat, then straightened up, sighing.

'Now I shan't be able to eat my dinner either,' she complained. 'Every time I see a dead body I get heartburn.'

'In that case, you'd better go home, lady.'

'Will you leave the coat on him?' asked the old woman, taking Mrs. Daniska's arm. Then, holding her skirt down with her other hand, she set off homewards again.

The men looked at each other. Another muffled shot was heard from a long way off in the direction of the Danube. Suddenly Uncle Janos bowed his fur-capped head and turned slowly away. 'Well!' gasped the soldier, raising his hand as if about to clap it to his brow; but his arm stopped half way. The two old women had disappeared in the shadow of the house. Only their slow splashing was still audible in

the night's quiet. The old porter wiped his sweating forehead with his red-checked handkerchief. 'That thieving old
witch ought to be burned!' he whispered, shaking his
head.

At home, the two old women were already in bed by the
time the men stole in one by one. Last to come was the lad
in the army blouse, but he too came empty-handed. Aunt
Mari, who had kept here eyes fixed on the door, raised her
eyebrows disapprovingly, then, with a determined movement,
she turned her back on the people assembled round the stove,
clattering plates and cutlery.

'So there you are,' she sighed, turning her mild, bespectacled gaze towards the wrinkled face of old Mrs. Daniska
who was lying next to her. 'And poor Uncle Ruzicska doesn't
have a decent rag to bless himself with . . .'

The old laundress folded her hands contentedly under the
blanket. 'And still they didn't do it!' she said. 'Yet Mr. Andrasi
could certainly do with a better overcoat to replace that thin
ragged coat he wears. But you see, dear, I've been doing the
washing and ironing for the best families for forty-four years,
and they put their laundry uncounted into my hands—I've
never pinched so much as a dirty handkerchief.'

'May God bless you for it,' the cobbler's widow said.

A thin wail rose from one corner—the rebellious complaint
of a ten day old child. Round the stove or squatting on the
edge of their beds, rather like sparrows, the old people were
noisily sipping the thick soup which had been distributed,
while in a corner, by the light of a candle, a heavy, grey-
haired woman, bending over a tub, was soaping her grandchild's pink bottom. Aunt Mari suddenly sat up in bed. 'Why,
have I ever taken anything?' she asked indignantly. 'It's
different if one person steals from someone else. But if a lot
of poor people steal together, it's as if God himself were
stealing!'

'Now don't take on so!' said the old laundress, lifting her hands defensively.

'And it's not as though they'd have been depriving anybody else!' continued Aunt Mari, her face flushing. 'May God rest the poor soul, but he's just lying there on the pavement with nobody to mourn him and tomorrow they'll put him in a hole. If we take that overcoat off him it's no more than if we were taking the skin off an old dead sheep.' Aunt Mari's spectacles flashed more and more severely. 'You see, Mrs. Daniska,' she continued, lowering her voice so as not to be overheard by the neighbours, 'I couldn't even eat my supper—I get so upset when I see a dead body. But do you think those gentlemen next door will bury him with that good overcoat on? Either they pull it off him or we do. Or rather, they will, now.'

The old laundress broke into unexpected laughter. 'But at least they'll work for it,' she giggled in her thin old voice; in the dark, it sounded like a small cracked bell. 'They were smart, those old fools, weren't they?'

Aunt Mari smiled. 'They landed them with our property,' she said, and with a quick movement she took off her spectacles and slipped them under her pillow. 'Now they'll have to do some work. That poor old man! Well, good night, Mrs. Daniska.'

She fell asleep quickly, but woke before dawn, and, resting her hand carefully on the side of the bed so as not to wake her neighbour, she sat up noiselessly. In the dim light of the night-lamp her eyes roamed over the cellar; the others were all asleep, their heavy snores jostled and entangled with each other under the low ceiling like an agitated curly-backed flock of sheep in a locked fold. Someone whimpered miserably in his sleep. From the next cellar one could hear the thin whistling snore of the retired postman. That's one we shall have to bury, thought Aunt Mari, lowering her feet carefully on to the cold stone floor. She pulled her spectacles from under her pillow and dressed quickly. She longed for some fresh air before the early morning bombing began.

As the front door was still locked, she walked round the yard for a bit, and then went up to her own flat on the third floor. The grey light of dawn had not yet suffused the coherent world outside, but when, a little later, she glanced out of the window to look up and down the street, she could distinguish clearly the hoarfrost-covered pavement with the outline of the dead body which had regained its original position under her window. Frightened, Aunt Mari clapped her hand to her mouth. 'They've put it back!' she thought, her heart beating. 'Upon my life, they've put it back!'

Gathering her skirts in both hands, she ran at breakneck speed down the stairs. In the air-raid shelter, people were beginning to wake up. Some were clearing their throats. Uncle Janos, his fur-capped head bent low, was pulling on his boots. At the creaking of the wooden door, every head turned towards the flushed and panting old woman who stood there in the open doorway. 'They've put it back!' she cried breathlessly. 'May Christ be my witness, they've put it back!'

'What?' asked the lame waiter, alarmed.

'The old gentleman.'

'What?' stammered the old porter. 'I don't understand.'

'They must have noticed, the scoundrels, and put it back during the night!' Aunt Mari cried angrily.

The entire cellar crowded round the excited old woman, the children screamed and jumped up on the benches. 'They've put it back! . . . they've put it back!' screeched the janitor's six-year-old son, shaking his rattle. Suddenly a sharp explosion shook the open door.

'Come in!' grumbled old Aunt Focher, a charwoman who was deaf in both ears. 'Keep away from the door, he can't get in that way!' But who it was that could not get in she did not vouchsafe.

As the gun-fire increased in intensity, going out into the street to inspect the situation was out of the question. The more loudly the women wailed, the more stubbornly silent the old men, outwitted, became; only the lame waiter seethed with indignation, and threatened the dark and oozing ceiling with his cane. The old porter stole out unnoticed from the shelter, and tramped up to Aunt Mari's flat.

The dead man, in his double-breasted overcoat, lay right under the window on the very edge of the pavement, in the exact spot from which they had dragged him the previous evening. The solicitor has returned my parcel, thought the old porter, and such bitterness welled up in him that he would have liked nothing better than to burst into tears. He leaned far out of the window, and stared at the next house.

'You'll pay for this, don't you worry!' he shouted angrily, shaking his old fist at the house. A flock of pigeons rose with a flurry of beating wings from the next-door roof, and, seconds later, in a cloud of smoke and dust, a shell slammed into the shuttered window of the corner grocery.

AUNT ANNA

ABOUT seven o'clock in the morning, both doors of the air-raid shelter flew silently open, and a heavy-framed old woman appeared on the threshold in the milky light. Her grey hair fluttered; she swung a small bundle in one hand, and the other hand she held pressed to her belly.

'Wake up!' she cried in her deep booming voice, like waves shifting pebbles on a beach. 'Wake up! The Flood's upon us!'

A night-light stood on a shelf fixed to the wall, and its flame swayed in the draught, casting a tiny yellow spot of radiance on the wall, no bigger than a rose-petal; however, it left dark the huge low-ceilinged cellar which connected with an even darker room at its farthest corner. The people snoring on beds, chairs, or divans, huddled close together, gradually stirred; here and there someone heaved himself half upright on one elbow, someone else yawned mightily, like a cat.

'Wake up!' cried the old woman, as she stood on the threshold, stretching her arm towards the sleeping people. 'May the Lord kick you out of your last resting place! How much longer are you going to idle away this black day?'

'What's happened?' screamed a woman.

A young girl sat up in bed and raised both hands to her head. Several people sneezed. Mr. Andrasi, the lame waiter, reached for his stick, and, flushing scarlet, brandished it at the ceiling. Aunt Mari, the cobbler's widow, produced the spectacles inherited from her husband from under her pillow

and put them on her nose; then, bending over the widow
Daniska who lay sleeping beside her, began gently to coax
her awake.

'What is it now?' Mrs. Daniska murmured. 'Have you
been dreaming about that horse again?'

'The Flood's upon us!' whispered Aunt Mari, bending over
the other widow's wrinkled face.

'Upon us?' the latter asked, still half asleep. She drew
her hand along her body, shook her head in negation, and
turned over on to her other side.

In the first cellar someone lit a candle. The tiny yellow
waves of its light were quick to interpret the unfolding outside
world. Half-clothed figures swayed in the semi-obscurity,
wrapped in shawls or dressed in trousers and shirts.

'What's happened? Who is she?' asked Mr. Polesz, an old
cabby who had only recently moved in after being bombed
out of his flat, pointing a finger at the massive, grey-haired
old woman at the door.

'That's Aunt Anna,' replied his brother, the retired postman. 'She lives on the second floor.'

'I've never seen her down here before,' grumbled the old
cabby.

'Well, she wouldn't leave her flat,' the postman explained.
'She says she isn't a rat, so why should she live in a cellar.'

'So why has she come down now?'

'What's happened?' quavered the woman who had
screamed.

'Jesus Christ, the Russians are here!' screeched another.

In a second the whole cellar was on its feet. The women
thronged with pale faces round the old woman who, pressing
one hand to her belly, and swinging her tiny bundle in the
other, stood motionless facing the excited crowd. Her black
crocheted shawl had slipped off her head, and the draught
stirred up the thick, iron-grey locks like a cloud of dust. The

age-old layers of the big-boned powerful face below remained
unmoved.

'Well, have you left your nests, my chickens?' she cried,
leaning her shoulder up against the door frame. 'Damn and
blast this lazy populace, snoring so loudly on Judgement Day
that it can't even hear the Angel's trumpet! Get a move on,
slaves, fetch water!'

'Is the house on fire, Aunt Anna?' yelled the pregnant
young woman in alarm, raising her hand defensively in front
of her body.

'Of course it isn't on fire, child,' said the old woman, her
face expressionless. 'I want a cup of coffee!'

Then she threw her bundle down on the floor, bent forward like a naughty little girl with her hands, palms downwards, on her knees, and broke into loud, mocking laughter
in her strong, masculine voice. Her big, bony frame swayed
backwards and forwards, the dry, clay layers of her face
threatened to crumble in this explosion of mirth; her eyes
sparkled.

'No, the house isn't on fire, girl,' she shouted, 'but I want
my coffee! Now—before the spring!' she added, in one of
her rare good moods, slapping her thigh with her hand. 'Mrs.
Daniska, I hear your potatoes have sprouted!'

'I haven't got a single potato, Aunt Anna,' she replied
startled.

'I thought you had,' murmured the old woman mockingly.
'No matter, you'll have enough next year if you live that
long!'

'God forgive you, Aunt Anna, but didn't you say the
Russians were here?' the old postman asked plaintively.

'I didn't,' the old woman shook her head.

'Then why did you come down?'

'Because they shot me out of my flat, daddy,' Aunt Anna
replied. 'The ceiling caved in on me—it's a miracle it didn't

crush me. But let's get a move on, my little birds. Stop preening yourselves and build a fire in that stove as if you were
building it on Mount Sinai!'

'The ceiling caved in?' Aunt Mari, the cobbler's widow
repeated in a shaky voice. 'Heavens, you might have been
killed, Aunt Anna!'

'So what?' said Aunt Anna in her thunderous voice. She
picked up her ridiculously small bundle from the floor, and
set off with creaking steps towards the stove in the inner
cellar. 'An electric furnace once exploded right beside me
at the factory, and nothing happened to me . . . Whose bed
am I going to sleep in?'

The two cellars were connected by a short narrow passage;
just before one turned into the passage, there was a small
recess opening out from the first cellar in which the most
distinguished inhabitants of the house, the widow and children of Councillor Pignitzky, nursed their delicate orphanhood
amidst the rough waves of the poor population surrounding
them. There was also a small stove in the recess for the
exclusive use of the Pignitzky's; the meals shared by the
rest of the cellar-dwellers were prepared by the women on
the large stove which stood in a corner of the inner cellar.
Apart from the Pignitzky's, only the janitor and his wife
lived on their own cooking—it was customary for her to
throw their meals together in their own ground-floor kitchen
during lulls, long or short, in the bombardment.

Aunt Anna stopped in front of the recess and pushed aside
the curtain which did duty for a door. 'Good morning,' she
said in a loud voice, her sharp grey eyes slowly scrutinising
the dim recess. 'Well, there's enough room here. I can sleep
on the couch with one child, and the other can share the bed
with its mother.'

'What does this woman want?' Mrs. Pignitzky cried, raising herself on one elbow, an alarmed expression on her face.

Aunt Anna threw up her head, and bent slightly forward. 'What does this woman want?' she repeated quietly. 'Only what is every woman's right before childbirth and death: a bed.'

'Do you want to have a child here?' asked Mrs. Pignitzky, startled.

Aunt Anna gazed at her and nodded her head twice, emphatically. But before the other woman, lying in bed, could open her mouth again, she released the curtain, turned her back on the inhabitants of the recess, and went abruptly back into the passage.

'Do even rats give themselves airs?' she cried, tramping noisily down between the two rows of beds towards the stove where an old laundress was chopping firewood with the shelter axe. 'Do the big rats still call the tune for the small rats to dance to before they all fry together in the fires of hell? Are there still big shots and small fry among the rats?'

'Hush, Aunt Anna,' said a tiny old woman who, trotting up behind her, grasped her arm. 'Leave her alone. She lost her husband less than a week ago.'

Aunt Anna stopped in her tracks, then, in slow motion like a lion, she turned round to face the diminutive charwoman who took an involuntary step backwards.

'What? . . . She lost her husband?' she asked in her booming voice. 'So, is there a single woman in this dump who hasn't lost her husband or won't lose her husband before she herself crawls under the ground? I raised four children myself without a husband . . . and here's one of them!'

She pointed to a lad aged about twenty wearing an army blouse, who was crouching on the edge of a bed munching a piece of dry bread.

'All right, mum, cease fire,' he said quietly. 'You don't have to eat the poor woman alive!'

'Shut up, you pipsqueak!' said the old woman, turning her

massive grey head towards her son. 'Did you ever see anything to beat that,' she growled indignantly. 'Have you ever
seen a rat getting up on its hindlegs and holding out its fore-
paws to be kissed? And have you ever seen another rat
crawling close and kissing them for it? Why don't you look
after your mother, you heartless creature, instead of hiding
behind your girl's skirts all day?'

The quiet cellar, with its peaceful herd of elderly men and
women, telling their beads, was brusquely catapulted out of
its normal rhythm by Aunt Anna's appearance. The gentle,
inward order of resignation, hitherto disturbed only by the
brutal outside events of the siege, disintegrated into its wild,
thorny elements and revealed its concealed fires. And as if
the world outside had only been waiting for this moment,
it seized the cellar, crouching in its fright, like a naughty
child its broken toy and hammered it.

An hour after Aunt Anna had moved in, a retreating
German machine-gun unit settled in one of the more protected areas of the house opening on to the courtyard—a little
tailor's shop—and one of their lorries backed into the front
door, blocking it so completely that one could reach the
street only by crawling out between the wheels and the wall.
The lorry was loaded with cases of ammunition, and if a
shell or a bomb had fallen near at hand, the explosion would
have blown the house up, and buried the cellar-dwellers
beneath its ruins.

During the morning, rumours began to circulate that the
Germans had no intention of vacating the tailor's shop, but
that, on the contrary, they were setting up a machine-gun
nest on a first floor balcony and, in case of close-range fight-
ing, would defend the building to their last bullet. The
members of a Rumanian labour detachment had been busy
for a week digging tank-traps at the corner of the street to
defend the line of retreat towards the Danube—this, too con-

firmed the rumours. But what was to happen to the inhabitants? Would the Germans evacuate the cellar?

The two old widows, Aunt Mari and Mrs. Daniska, were shelling beans for dinner, sitting on the edge of their beds with a white tea-towel spread across their knees. Mrs. Daniska's hands were shaking so much that the beans jumped from her fingers like fleas.

'Where are they going to put us then?' she complained. 'The cellars in the other houses round about are so crowded already that there isn't room for another person in them. And where am I to put my bed where I've slept for forty years to save it from being blown up?'

Aunt Mari nodded seriously; her spectacles slipped down the ridge of her nose. 'Perhaps they won't evacuate us,' she said. 'They can't chase so many people out into the streets, can they?'

'I've heard,' went on Mrs. Daniska, 'about a house in the Ferenc district where the German's didn't evacuate the inhabitants, but just settled down with them in the cellar, and the Russians threw grenades down the airshafts. Just imagine a grenade like that falling on my bed!'

'It may not fall on yours, dear . . .' Aunt Mari comforted her. 'Who told you this? Was it Mr. Polisz?'

'It was.'

'He should know better than to go making people nervous,' Aunt Mari grumbled. 'Where has that soft-witted old porter got to?'

As the old porter was the only one in the cellar who spoke some German they sent him in deputation to the occupying forces to find out what they intended to do with the house, the fatherland and their lives. In the interests of greater emphasis, prestige and appearance, Mr. Andrasi, the lame waiter, and the shelter commander accompanied him. A whole hour went by, and there was still no sign of them.

'Come nearer, dear,' Mrs. Daniska signalled to the other
widow. 'I want to tell you something.'

In the eight years since fate had thrown them together in
their one room and kitchen flat on the third floor, the two
women had become so familiar with each other that each
knew the other's reaction to situations in advance: like the
shadow of a familiar object before a known source of light.
Once again Aunt Mari knew exactly what her co-tenant
wanted to talk about.

'Aunt Anna?' she asked, nodding her head.

'It's that old witch who's brought the Germans down on
us!' whispered the widow Daniska.

The other woman looked up startled. 'What do you mean?'

'I don't know,' said the laundress, 'but you'll see, she'll
bring misfortune to the whole cellar. The moment she came
in the world went dark round me . . . and this is a bad sign,
a hunch which has never let me down yet.'

'But you were asleep, Mrs. Daniska!' Aunt Mari cried
indignantly. 'I could hardly shake you awake!'

The old laundress ignored this piece of evidence. 'She picks
a quarrel with everybody,' she whispered, and her mild face
flushed with anger. 'She sets everybody at everybody else's
throat. There's no order in her. She loves neither God nor
man.'

'Who is her son's girl, do you know?' Aunt Mari enquired.
'I know.'

Aunt Mari awaited a continuation of this reply in silence.
As it was not forthcoming, she reached up and tied the kerchief round her head. 'I wonder why there's been no raid
today?' she said tactfully.

'And that's another bad sign,' Mrs. Daniska replied. 'They
save it all up and then come down on us like a cloud of
wasps.'

Suddenly, both fell silent. Arriving back from the courtyard, the delegation entered the cellar, and at the same moment, like a musical accompaniment, a succession of mighty explosions crashed in through the entrance, surrounding the delegation with an aureole, and increasing its stature.

'Nothing doing,' announced the old porter, scratching his nose. 'We can't get a word out of them. They say we're just to keep calm, and they'll warn us in time if we have to evacuate the cellar. They'll give us at least two hours."

'Good God, two hours!' cried the pregnant young woman, throwing up her hands. 'How are we to get ready in two hours with the children and food and things? And where do they intend to move us to?'

'Oh, my bed!' sighed Mrs. Daniska.

'They're whacked,' the old porter continued, 'so whacked that they just threw themselves down on the floor—they didn't even eat their rations. Their officer comes from Berlin.'

A long shadow appeared on the wall; the small group was suddenly plunged in darkness. Someone had stepped in front of the night-light.

'Don't make yourself so important, you wrinkled old busy-body!' grumbled Aunt Anna who had been asleep on one of the bunks, quiet and motionless, ever since she moved down to the cellar in the morning, and now suddenly came to life at the sound of gunfire. 'Who wants to know where your officer comes from?'

Abashed, the old porter fell silent.

'We'll have to move out in two hours, Aunt Anna, and I don't know where to,' the lame waiter told her.

'So what?' boomed the old woman. 'I moved out of my flat in ten minutes. That's how long it took me to crawl out from under the rubble.'

'Anna dear, perhaps you could go up and talk to the commander,' the widow suggested slyly. 'Say that this place is full of old people and invalids, so perhaps they'd better move next door.'

'Damn you!' yelled the old woman furiously. Then she burst out laughing; she laughed happily, boisterously, like a child, her grey locks shaking round her massive head. 'You're a one, Mrs. Daniska, you are . . . !' she shouted, with a flash of her big yellow teeth. 'You want me to go up and ask them, do you? Do you know, my little pigeon, when I last asked a favour from anyone? Forty years ago, when I asked my mother to give me a clean nightgown for my wedding night! And never since, even though I brought four children into the world and buried two of them.'

She was silent for a second, and passed her gaunt, bony fist over her forehead. 'That they should get out of here because the house is full of old people and invalids?' she repeated after a while. 'Should I send them to the young and healthy, Mrs. Daniska, my dove, so that they can disable them too? No, my little birds! If we had to make war, we must perish ourselves!'

'I didn't make this war!' cried Mrs. Daniska indignantly.

'So what did you do?' replied Aunt Anna indifferently, switching her sharp, grey eyes from one wrinkled face to the other. 'Was there just one single woman in this saintly herd who forbade her husband or son to go off soldiering? If we women had shut up shop, the men couldn't have made war— not on their lives! Now, of course, that they have shot both our husbands and our sons from our beds it's no use moaning. Too late for that, my little birds. But my son won't go to war as long as I live.'

About four o'clock in the afternoon, the Germans moved out with their ammunition lorries. But no sooner had the excitement stirred up in their hearts by this unexpected pleasure settled down again—and their joy was so immoderate that Mr. Polesz, the cabby from the Ferenc district, had jumped into the middle of the cellar where he proceeded to do a dance, snapping his fingers, while in the corner, an old laundress retched convulsively over a pail—no sooner had the fun and games calmed down, than another alarming rumour came to upset their short-lived peace. About six o'clock the janitor returned from the street with the news that an Arrow-cross unit consisting of eight or ten men had taken up quarters in the next house, armed to the teeth with tommy-guns, rifles and hand grenades.

Just as flies buzz more loudly and sting more venomously in the autumn, before they die—as if quarrelling with death —so did the Arrow-cross men roam the martyred town in the last weeks of the siege, hitting out even more and destroying their opponents with increasing barbarity. During the day they hunted for deserters, and at night they murdered the Jews; in the mornings, the flag-stones on the bank of the Danube, especially round the bridge-heads, shone black with the blood of the victims. As soon as it was dark, and the besieging guns fell silent, the stillness of the deserted streets began to resound with the rattle of machine-guns.

'There's a raid on next door,' the janitor announced, twirling his thick grey moustache nervously. 'Then we can obviously expect them, as they haven't been here yet.'

There were no Jews in the house, but there was a deserter. Aunt Anna's son had been sitting round in the cellar for eight days now with a faked furlough pass. He had shed his army blouse when the Germans came—the old postman took it and lent the lad his old jacket instead. But what would have been protection enough against the Germans would obviously not satisfy the Arrow-cross men.

'Give me a piece of bread, Mum,' the lad said, 'I'll disappear for a while.'

'Where are you going to hide, child?' asked Mrs. Daniska in a shaky voice.

'What do you want to know that for?' growled Aunt Anna, taking her last piece of bread from her little bundle. 'Why should everybody be in the secret? I don't know either, but you don't hear me asking!'

The lad put his face close to the widow Daniska's ear, whispered something, then he laughed, turned round and ran out of the shelter. The old woman stared after him, horrified.

'Even at a time like this he can crack jokes,' she whispered.

Mr. Andrasi, the lame waiter, went out to stand watch at the street door. But when, half an hour later he came back in, chilled to the bone, he had no fresh news about the raiding party which was still busy in the next building.

'It's no use standing out there,' said Aunt Mari, 'time enough to find out when they're here!'

'Let them come!' said an elderly charwoman whom the cellar—since she spent the whole day warm in her bed—had almost completely cured of her chronic rheumatism, 'Let them come, there are no Jews here!'

They had a thick soup for dinner and some lentils left over from noon. People gathered round the stove, sitting on bunks and on the edges of beds, but the food went down no more easily than it had at noon, while the Germans were still in the house: nobody asked for a second helping. Nor did any-one feel like going to bed: what was the use of falling asleep if the raid would wake them up anyway? Only Aunt Anna retired immediately after dinner. The pregnant young woman, who had been sleeping in a bed by herself because of her condition, moved over and made room for her. The old woman's sleep was as quiet as her body was big; she slept deeply and without moving, like a child, and there was a good chance that she would not disturb her hostess. Her old brown furrowed face rested peacefully in the delicate light of the candle, like bread wrapped in a cloth.

Towards midnight, however, by the time the Arrow-cross
men marched into the cellar, everybody was asleep, and the
startled faces, slowly shedding the bark of sleep, stared like
livid masks into the zig-zagging beams of the torches. The
wind came whistling through the open door; a man next
to the wall broke into low sobs.

'Light a candle!' shouted one of the Arrow-cross men in
a hoarse, thin treble.

There were three of them; an elderly, moustachioed man
wearing a green hunting hat with a feather, and two short,
pale, dark-haired boys. All three wore Arrow-cross arm-bands,
and carried a number of red-handled hand-grenades in their
belts. They looked like children going to the playground with
their tutor.

'Are there any Jews here?' screeched one in a penetrating
voice. 'Out of bed and have your papers ready!'

The light of the candle flickered in the second cellar. Aunt
Mari bent over the widow Daniska and tugged at her pink
flannel nightgown.

'Wake up,' she said in a low voice so as not to alarm the
old woman. 'We have guests!'

'What's up now? Why are you bothering me?' the laundress murmured. 'Can't you see I'm shelling my beans?'

Before she could turn over on to her other side, Aunt Mari
pulled the blanket off her. 'Stop cooking!' she said angrily.
'Where are your papers?'

Mrs. Daniska sat up in bed. 'Tell me, dear,' she said, her
voice shaking with indignation, 'are you determined not to
let me sleep? The whole cellar is my witness that you wake
me night after night on some pretext or other...'

One of the Arrow-cross men blocked the door with a
tommy-gun in his hand, the elderly man in the hunting cap
sat down at the small table near the entrance, and the third
walked slowly along between the beds shining his torch into

the faces of the men and women as they hurriedly dressed. The silence was so absolute that the janitor's little daughter woke up and started crying.

The shelter commander and the janitor stood in front of the table. 'Total?'

'Forty-seven.'

'Jews?'

'No, sir,' replied the porter.

The elderly man drew his hand across his forehead with a tired gesture.

'If we do find a deserter or a foreign national, we'll take you both,' he said in a low voice. 'You can still change your mind.'

'There aren't any, sir,' repeated the porter. 'Only poor people live in this house.'

The man who had examined both cellars with a torch returned to the table. 'Forty-three,' he reported.

'Four missing.'

'Have you been in the recess as well?' asked Uncle Janos, the shelter commander.

The short, dark Arrow-cross man departed and came back a moment later. 'One woman and two children,' he announced in high pitched shrill voice. 'Forty-three and three, in fact.'

'That's still one short.'

'There's a soldier who is at the front,' said the janitor.

The elderly man closed his eyes as if yielding to sudden exhaustion. 'Why have you still got him on your list?' he asked after a while in an ever lower voice. 'If he doesn't live here, strike him off your list.'

'He used to stay here with his mother,' the janitor said.

The elderly man made a note on the sheet of paper lying in front of him.

'Any other premises here?'

'No.'

'You're lying!' the elderly man said, quietly. 'I saw seven or eight doors at the end of the corridor. Coal cellars?'

'Yes,' said the janitor, flushing.

'Those are counted as premises too,' the Arrow-cross man explained. 'Now, send me in first the women, then the men, one by one, with their papers.'

The short young man with the effeminate voice went to the back of the cellar. One by one the women presented themselves at the table; the pale dark girl who slept in the bed opposite the door turned faint with excitement, and had to sit down on a chair. When Aunt Anna announced her name the elderly man mused for a while, his head bent, fiddling with his pencil. He had a thick gold pencil.

'Are you that soldier's mother?' he asked.

The old woman seemed to shrink, her booming voice became soft and melodious, her face gentle and sweet. 'Yes, sir,' she replied, 'I have a soldier son.'

'Where is he?'

'If only I knew!' the old woman sighed. 'Last week I had a post-card from him, but it didn't tell me where he was. If only I knew whether he is still alive!'

The elderly man nodded aprovingly as if he were satisfied with her answer. 'Toddle over to the wall, aunty,' he said. 'Over there near the door, not with the others.'

The old woman's face twitched almost imperceptibly. 'Yes, sir,' she said. The pale dark-haired girl pressed her hand to her mouth and gave a low moan. The elderly man turned his head in her direction, looked her over carefully, and then bent over his papers. He questioned two more women and then turned back to the girl.

'You go and stand by the wall too,' he said quietly. 'There, next to the old woman. And be quick about it!'

Half an hour later, when he had finished with the men, he

motioned to the young Arrow-cross man, standing at the back of the cellar, to join him. They talked in low voices so that nobody could catch a word of what they were saying. The young Arrow-cross man went out through the door. The elderly man leaned back in his chair, stretched his legs out, took his gun from its holster and put it down on the table. He sat quite still, his head thrown back, until the Arrow-cross man returned, accompanied by another one; in front of them they pushed Aunt Anna's soldier son. The lad's hands were tied behind his back, and his face and hands were covered in a thick layer of coal-dust.

The pregnant young woman hid her face in her hands and screamed.

'Be quiet! I don't want to hear a cheep out of you!' screeched the shrill-voiced, short Arrow-cross man. The janitor's face suddenly went livid and he took an involuntary step backwards.

'Where is that furlough pass?' asked the elderly man.

'In my pocket,' the lad replied in a low voice.

'Take it out for him!'

The short Arrow-cross man reached into the soldier's breast-pocket and pulled out a folded sheet of paper. The elderly man took a look at it and then tore it up with deliberate movements. 'It's faked,' he said wearily.

The soldier did not answer. The Arrow-cross man standing next to him prodded him in the ribs with the butt of his tommy-gun. 'Can't you answer?'

'What can I say?' the soldier growled. 'It isn't faked.'

'Is that why you hid out there in the coal?' the elderly man asked him.

'I hid so you shouldn't arrest me,' the soldier said. 'And so you shouldn't tear up my furlough pass.'

The dark haired girl standing by the wall burst into loud sobs. The candle in the second cellar went out.

'Why have you put out that candle, you bunch of bastards!' the Arrow-cross man by the door yelled. 'Light it, or I'll let you have it!'

'It's burnt out!' cried a shaky, old, female voice. 'Will you please wait until I light another?'

'It's burnt out . . .' said the elderly man thoughtfully. 'Send me that little old man there.' He raised his arm, and slowly pointed to the retired postman squatting on one of the beds at the back of the cellar between Mr. Andrasi, the lame waiter, and the old porter. The postman immediately rose and walked up to the table.

'Where did you get that army blouse?' the elderly man asked him.

'From him,' the old man muttered.

'Did you swap?'

'We swapped.'

'Why?' the elderly man asked, looking into the postman's face from under half-closed eyes.

'Why?' the postman shouted. 'Because I've had enough of this war!'

For a moment there was silence.

'Don't!' the elderly man said to the short, shrill-voiced Arrow-cross man who had raised his arm to hit the old man. 'What did you say?'

'I said, with no disrespect to you intended,' the postman answered, flushing, 'that this snot-nose had better not touch me or I'll kick his guts out as surely as my name is Karoly Csukas.'

The two Arrow-cross men standing by the table laughed loudly. But not a muscle moved in the elderly man's face.

'We shan't lay a finger on you,' he said. His voice sounded more and more tired. 'We shan't touch you, but we shall execute you. Go and stand by the wall.'

Before the old man could move, Aunt Anna, who had

been standing with her back up against the wall motionless, watching her son with eyes which contracted like a cat's, took two long strides towards the table. She bent her massive torso forward, and stared into the elderly man's face.

'Are you going to shoot my son too?' she asked in her deep voice.

'Draw your horns in,' the elderly man murmured, while the two Arrow-cross men pulled the old woman back by her arms. 'What's happened? Have you grown? A moment ago you looked a lot smaller.'

'Even the corn on my toe is bigger than you, you bastard!' the old woman said.

The dark-haired, pale young girl by the wall began to slide slowly down until she was sitting on the ground.

'What's getting you all worked up, Aunty?' said the elderly man. 'We won't shoot you—you're only the mother!'

When the two Arrow-cross men took the soldier and the postman between them, and began to herd them towards the door, Aunt Anna sprang after them. She kicked one in the leg, and turned the other one towards her by the shoulder to rake his face with her long, bony fingers. 'Run!' she cried hoarsely. A gun went off behind them. The soldier jumped through the door.

The Arrow-cross man whom Aunt Anna had kicked lay on the ground on his belly, whilst the other fingered, whining, his bleeding eyes and face. Aunt Anna slipped slowly sideways, then fell heavily to the ground. More shots were heard from the lobby, and then from the yard. In the second cellar someone groaned.

*   *   *

Towards morning, before she died, the old woman regained consciousness for an hour.

'My little birds,' she said, 'you're about as brave as dry
goat's droppings. Yet it doesn't become the old to be cowardly.
The young still hope for happiness, but what have we, the
old, got to lose? We've been deserted by God and man, we
are alone with our unwanted love, our hopes have fallen by
the wayside, so why not show some dignity before we breathe
out our souls? We have lived in ignominy ever since we first
opened our eyes, those of us who possess anything stole it,
those who don't lick bottoms in order to gain; we never gave
nor received any gift on this stinking earth except a child
in our wombs or a rope round our necks. And now, when
you were offered this cheap opportunity, because you were
standing on the brink of your graves anyway, you missed
even that, my little birds. He who has kept his eyes on profit
all his life, and cannot pull himself together even at the last
moment to bring his blurry eye back into focus, deserves the
hell he has invented for himself. You'll die as uselessly as you
lived. I've spent half a lifetime in this house and if, during
that time I had found only one person who stood up on his
hind-legs—and that only once, I'd say: all right, I forgive
you for having been born. But even the best among you
claim salvation on the grounds that you have neither cheated
nor stolen. The good were good because they arranged a
pillow under someone's head, the brave were brave because
they held out their other cheek to be slapped, the loyal were
loyal because they didn't bite their mothers' ankle when she
turned her back on them—but that's all there was to your
virtue. Everyone here lay low quietly in the warm dung so
as not to catch cold. Yet the poor have duties to perform.
I'll say it out loud so you can hear me! Because only the
poor know what misery is, it is up to them to protect the
others from it. Because the poor alone need God, let them
reject him! Because their lives aren't worth a fig, let them
give them away! Because the poor hear no other music than

the rattling of their chains, let them rattle those chains until
their unborn children's eardrums burst with it! Do you
think, my little birds, that because you cover each other up,
share your rations, and put up with each other's bad smell,
you have paid creation even that one measly onion it claims
in taxes?'

FEAR

THE River Lethe does not run past the front doors of the houses on Nador Street. Descending the double spiral staircase to the cellar-underworld of the apartment building, the widow Daniska carried on her sandals the live dust of the street. The terrestrial dust brought the underworld alive and turned it into hell. Ceaselessly, memory sent down its sulphurous flashes of lightning.

The widow Daniska looked around blinking in hell.

'Are you asleep, Aunt Mari?' she asked after a while.

'Why should I be asleep?' the woman addressed replied. 'Why should I be asleep in broad daylight when I can't even sleep at night?'

The two widows had moved together about a week before from the air raid shelter of their tottering house to the cellar of the neighbouring Nador Street building. Apart from their memories, they had saved only their bedding and two red saucepans from among the smoking ruins that had buried the eight years of their common past. Fortunately they had landed in a more or less familiar environment. Mrs. Daniska had been going out to wash and iron and Aunt Mari to clean the well-to-do homes of the neighbourhood and thus they were not short of high-class acquaintances. Mr. Finiasz, the council secretary, and his family gave the two old women a little cold food in the evenings. Lawyer Bor's wife offered them white bread with caraway seeds and an occasional cup of tea, not to speak of other good-hearted cellar-dwellers . . .

'If you are not asleep, Aunt Mari,' the widow Daniska went on, 'then tell me who that man standing at the door is. He never takes his eyes off me!'

The tiny old woman turned her eyes towards the gaunt, bearded young man standing at the door but her wrinkled, mild face, like a dim mirror, remained unaffected by the sight.

'I don't know him,' she mumbled. 'But if I look more closely,' she added slipping her spectacles down to the point of her nose and scanning the young man at the door once more with her naked blue gaze, 'if I look more closely it seems to me as if I've seen him before.'

'I never have,' declared Mrs. Daniska, 'but as far as I can see in this God-forsaken darkness, he seems to be waving to me.'

'Or to me,' the cobbler's widow opined. 'Shall we go and look?'

'If you want to.'

'Well, why doesn't he come here if he wants to talk to me?' murmured Aunt Mari with sudden suspicion and her clear, old face darkened.

From the corner of her eye she threw a quick glance at the long-necked, fur-coated woman sitting on the bed next to hers who stared motionless in front of her, her hands resting in her lap. Every time the dull, hissing sound of an exploding bomb penetrated from the landing, a nervous twitch rippled over her thin, big-eyed bird's face, like a small wave over the surface of water. Since eight in the morning, when the air raid began, she had never for a moment lifted her straight glance from the vision of death. 'In a quarter of an hour they'll shut off the water in No. 12, dear lady,' an elderly man next to her said, 'if they don't stop by then we shan't be cooking lunch today.'

The widow Daniska suddenly rose and set out towards the door to the landing.

'Come along, Aunt Mari,' she called back.

They had to make their tortuous way between two rows of beds to get to the door. The huge cellar, propped up in all its length by thick posts, was illuminated by a single small night-light; the oblique shadows of the posts divided the uncertain semi-obscurity into wavering sections in which the figures, squatting motionless side by side seemed like the letters of an obituary. Whenever the door leading into the neighbouring cellar was opened the coats hanging at the feet of the beds fluttered in the draught and chased the flee-ing shadow of a line across the huge room.

'Come out to the landing, Mrs. Daniska,' the bearded young man at the door said when the two widows reached him and, without waiting for their reply, he turned and walked out through the door.

The landing was deserted but somewhat lighter than the cellar; a little sunshine seeped in from the stairs leading to the yard.

'Don't start moaning,' said the young man hoarsely, 'and, what is more important still, don't call me by my name. Are there any Arrow-cross men in the cellar?'

'No,' replied Aunt Mari in a shaky voice. The widow Daniska crossed herself.

'Take me some place where we can be alone,' the young man murmured. 'And hurry up, I want to sit down.'

'You want to sit down?' Mrs. Daniska repeated, surprised.

'Let's go,' the young man said. Aunt Mari led the way. A narrow, low-ceilinged corridor opened from the landing and ran along the private coal-cellars with their locked iron doors and ended at the central heating furnace, which was surrounded by a wooden fence. The young man switched on his torch. In the corridor, the boom of the guns was louder and one could clearly distinguish the nervous clatter of the fighter planes' machine-guns.

'I've had bad luck with the coal once already,' the young man murmured sweeping the beam of his torch round the furnace room; the billowing coal-mounds sparkled black in the rays of the electric light. 'The Arrow-cross pulled me out of one coal cellar. Aren't there any here?'

He threw himself down on the coal.

'Don't people come in here?' he asked stretching out his legs. 'If this place is safe I could stay here until nightfall.'

The widow Daniska broke into loud sobs. The young man immediately put out his torch.

'Shut up, or I'm on my way,' he growled. 'I haven't slept for three days. When did your house collapse?'

'It's a week ago today,' Aunt Mari replied. 'It was hit by a big bomb in the morning and another one at noon.'

'The day after your mother's death . . .' sighed the widow Daniska wiping her eyes.

'Is my mother dead?' the young man asked.

'She is, child,' Aunt Mari answered.

The coal began to roll from under the young man's boots, a few lumps jumped with a thud against the iron wall of the furnace. 'Jesus Christ!' he swore, 'can't you keep quiet?'

He bent forward, the muscles of his face tensed, his chin jutting forward; but his ear caught no alarming sound. His eyes had become used to the darkness, to his right and left the swaying shadows of the two old women emerged undulating from the denser darkness of the coal.

'How did she die?' he asked curtly.

'The Arrow-cross men shot her dead,' Aunt Mari replied, 'the moment you jumped through the door.'

'I heard the shots,' the young man growled. 'I thought they were firing after me.'

Aunt Mari shook her head.

'There were two shots, weren't there?'

'Two.'

Another lump of coal slid out from under the young man's boot but this time he didn't notice.

'Then I heard right,' he said after a little while. 'I heard two shots, almost simultaneously. I thought they were shooting after me . . . Are there no Arrow-cross men here?'

'No, there aren't, child,' said Aunt Mari.

'Are you sure?'

'They wouldn't recognize you anyway,' the widow Daniska whispered in a barely audible voice, 'even we ourselves didn't recognize you at first. We both wondered, Aunt Mari and I, whether it was to us the strange, bearded young man was waving.'

'Don't chatter, Mrs. Daniska,' the young man said. 'I didn't ask you whether they would recognize me or not, but whether there are any of them here or not. Can't you give me a straight answer?'

'There aren't any,' the old woman replied patiently.

The young man sighed. Aunt Mari stared silently in front of her in the thick coal-dusty darkness, her knees shaking.

'Wouldn't you like to eat something, child?' she asked pressing her hand to her breast.

'I wouldn't mind,' the young man said absent-mindedly. 'I haven't eaten for three days except for a few raw carrots. What is there to eat?'

In quick succession two ear-splitting explosions penetrated into the cellar from the direction of the yard; the air was filled with thick coal-dust.

'That one was next door,' the young man said coughing. 'They are strafing this neighbourhood. I was almost hit by one last night.'

'Where?' the widow asked.

'On the corner, among the ruins,' the young man coughed again. 'That's where I hide out nights but I can't sleep for

the cold. If I could stay here tonight . . . I haven't slept for
three nights . . .'

The two old women were silent.

'So my mother is dead,' the young man said after a while.
'One could say that she died in my place, couldn't one? I
was the deserter and she was shot dead. How old was she?'

'Sixty-four,' Aunt Mari said. 'When were you born?'

The young man made no reply, he was obviously thinking.
The widow Daniska shifted her weight from one leg to the
other, the crumbling coal crackled beneath her feet. From
afar, towards the other end of the corridor, they heard the
creak of an iron door being opened.

'When were you born?' Aunt Mari asked in a louder voice.

For a while they waited for the answer, then both turned
carefully round and, on tiptoe, groping, their arms out-
stretched, they set out towards the corridor. They were followed by slow, even snores. Mrs. Daniska shuddered.

'He fell asleep,' she told herself aloud and shook her head
in amazement. 'He fell asleep, Aunt Mari!'

Reaching the lighter corridor, both stopped.

'The janitor's assistant belongs to the Arrow-cross,' Aunt
Mari said. 'He must not know or he would denounce him.'

'Mr. Finiasz, the council secretary is also an Arrow-cross
man,' replied the widow Daniska.

When they came to the bend in the corridor they stopped
again. Aunt Mari leaned her back against the wall.

'Dr. Bor, the lawyer, is one of them too,' she declared.

'What's the name of that long-necked woman sitting beside you?' Mrs. Daniska asked.

'Mrs. Milos,' Aunt Mari murmured. 'She belongs to them
too.'

'The janitor is also an Arrow-cross man,' the widow
Daniska said and burst out crying afresh.

Reaching the landing, the two old women stopped again.

Aunt Mari waited patiently until her friend's emotion had abated, then she took her own handkerchief and tenderly wiped away the tears from around the old laundress's nose.

'The assistant janitor steals coal from the furnace room,' she said. 'I saw him yesterday, he was taking away two pailfuls.'

'Then he will find the boy,' Mrs. Daniska cried.

Another falling bomb shook the walls. Inside, a piece of plaster dropping from the ceiling fell on the head of the lawyer's little daughter, scratching her forehead. For a while the company assembled round the lawyer's bed remained silent, only the frightened sobs of the child were audible in the corner.

'They've reached Andrassy Avenue already,' said the lawyer. 'The Pest side is finished.'

'Karoly, I beg you, let's cross over to Buda before it is too late!' whispered his wife, a powerfully built, round-faced woman with flashing white teeth and bushy brows meeting at the root of her nose. 'We'd all be comfortable in my mother's house.'

'I'm not going,' said the lawyer.

Mr. Finiasz, the council secretary who, having no bed, slept in a green leather armchair between his wife's divan and the lawyer's bed, sniggered.

'I'd go if I were you,' he grumbled. 'We'll have nothing to laugh about when the Russians get here.'

'If they get here!'

'Two more days at most,' the lawyer said and his putty-coloured face twitched.

'Are you going to try your luck, my dear colleague?'

The lawyer shrugged.

'Karoly, I beg you ...'

'Either it comes off or it doesn't,' her husband said looking around blinking. 'For they'd catch up with us not only in

Buda but in Germany as well, my good Finiasz. What are you hoping for?'

Someone from the next cellar threw open the connecting wooden door, stopped for a moment on the threshold, looked around and, reassured, retreated.

'It didn't drop here,' announced a retired colonel three beds further off, who, though he was hard of hearing, accompanied all ballistic events with pronouncements that allowed no appeal. Tiny pieces of plaster fell from the ceiling onto the beds.

'God almighty!' screamed a female voice in a remote corner of the cellar, 'I can't stand it any longer!'

Nobody moved. A bespectacled old woman broke into low sobs.

'Damn that bitch!' said Mrs. Finiasz, a short, dark, mouse-faced woman, aloud. 'She has a ton of potatoes in the cellar but she wouldn't let anyone have even a single one.'

The Red Cross nurse of the cellar rose reluctantly, her face stormy, from the edge of her bed and revived the unconscious woman with some vinegar. But less than fifteen minutes later the swan-necked Mrs. Milos was also in need of the vinegar sponge.

Mrs. Milos sat next to the lawyer on a low stool between the two beds, wrapped in her fur-coat, her head bent, listening motionless to the conversation that sped back and forth above her. When, at times, she raised her eyes from the grey concrete floor where she searched for the never-to-be dreams of a different world, her shining, metallic glance crept up to Mr. Finiasz's angular, sanguine face, alighted on it for a second, then returned hurriedly to her underworld visions. It seemed at such times as if her body changed its tone, it tensed, her neck flushed, her beautiful, pearly teeth flashed ecstatically between her lusty, painted lips. The town clerk turned his face away.

'Either it comes off or it doesn't. For they'd catch up with us not only in Buda but in Germany as well, my good Finiasz. What are you still hoping for?'—he heard the lawyer's voice.

Mrs. Milos threw back her head, her eyes rested for a second on the town clerk's face, her knees parted a little. Her lips moved but her words remained inaudible because the sudden explosion and the screams of the woman in the corner suppressed all other sounds.

'She has a ton of potatoes in the cellar but she wouldn't give anyone even one,' repeated Mrs. Finiasz who, with her grey, mousy face and skinny body was as unsuited to her powerfully built husband as the fragrance of hay is unlikely to fill the stomach of a hungry ox. Mrs. Milos shook her head mechanically. The damp air of the cellar grew even heavier from the smell of vinegar.

'God almighty, I can't stand any more of this!' screamed the woman in the corner, 'It is driving me mad!'

Mrs. Milos raised her head again.

'What do you think,' she asked the lawyer, 'do I have to vacate my flat if the Russians come in?'

'Was it a Jewish flat?'

The woman nodded silently.

'Probably,' the lawyer said, 'though it obviously depends also on whether or not the former owner returns.'

'I don't even know them.'

The council secretary laughed.

'You'll get acquainted when they return.'

'And if they don't?' asked the woman turning away her head and addressing her words to the lawyer as if she had not heard the council secretary's malicious laughter.

'Why shouldn't they return?' the lawyer grumbled irritably. 'As soon as we leave they'll break out of the ghetto like wild animals. Unless . . .'

'Unless the ghetto gets blown up first?' asked the woman hoarsely. 'Isn't that so?'

'And if it does get blown up,' said the council secretary after a while. 'One specimen of the breed is certain to survive and he, my dear lady, will make you pay for all seven of Christ's wounds!'

Mrs. Milos raised her bird's face, suddenly it was burning, her dim glance assumed a new sparkle.

'Me?' she cried raspingly, 'Why, what harm did I do them? Did I send them to the ghetto? I moved into an empty flat allotted to me by the authorities. Is it my fault if . . .'

'Calm yourself!' the lawyer said.

But Mrs. Milos paid no heed to the warning. She pulled herself slowly up from the stool and, smoothing down her narrow hips with her two palms, spreading her feet wide and bending her waist slightly forward she turned with her entire body towards the council secretary.

'What do you have against me?' she asked almost humbly. 'Why do you torment me?'

'What do you mean?' asked the man flushing and threw a quick glance at his wife.

Mrs. Milos closed her eyes.

'Will they put me out of the flat?'

'Stop fretting, Ilonka,' said the lawyer with increasing irritation. 'Just at present we don't even know whether there'll be any flat left . . . or if you'll ever enter it alive. If they go on like this we shall all burn to cinders in this hell.'

This time the bomb must have hit the house itself: the ground rose beneath their feet, dust exuded from the walls, a glass rolled with a loud clatter from the table. The lawyer's wife grasped the edge of the bed with both hands.

'So I shall be put out of my flat,' repeated Mrs. Milos. 'And who will pay me back what I spent on having it cleaned and redecorated? You, who allotted it to me?'

'I?' said the council secretary aghast.

Suddenly the woman clapped both hands to her face and threw herself full length down on the bed. In a second the storm of weeping dissolved the severe discipline of her narrow body, her limbs jerked wildly, the way a tree whips in a whirlwind, her belly rose immodestly above her loins, her neck writhed as if it wanted to tear itself from her body, one unlaced shoe flew off her foot. The shadow of unconsciousness painted her face dark. It took more than half an hour before the fit passed and her wild yells, that upset the whole cellar, abated. From her fainting spell she slid without transition into deep sleep.

By then, the cannonade had ceased; the cellar emptied quickly, only the children remained underground—watched over by a few women—and an old woman in mourning who spoke with a German accent and her son who had moved in from one of the neighbouring houses. The ventilating shaft was opened, the women began to sweep. The fresh, soaked wood crackled loudly in the large stove. The assistant janitor brought two pails of water from the next house where the water supply had been turned on for an hour because of the morning air raid.

'Is that all?' asked the lawyer's wife, air-raid warden of the building, when she saw the man placing the two pails near the stove and getting ready to chop wood.

The man shrugged.

'Why, this isn't even enough for the cooking,' the woman said. 'We need two more pails in the lavatory.'

'I won't get to the tap again,' the assistant janitor grumbled, 'half the street is out there and at twelve sharp they are cutting it off.'

'Don't answer back!' the woman said sharply.

By the time the man returned with the two pails of water, Mrs. Bor was no longer in the cellar. The man slammed down

the two pails swearing; half the water splashed out. His face
was bathed in perspiration.

'That sort wants shutting up in a ghetto too,' he said, his
back bent, his narrow eyes above the wide cheekbones burning with hatred. 'They are no better than the Jews when it
comes to exploiting us, God damn them!'

The widow Daniska who was on her knees, busy wiping
up the spilled water turned her mild, reddened face to the
man.

'You must not swear, Uncle Peter,' she said kindly. 'It'll
make you neither wiser nor fatter.'

'But he is right,' put in one of the sweeping women.
'Because it wouldn't hurt Her Ladyship to do a hard day's
work.'

'She might lose weight,' said another woman.

The assistant janitor who had been standing motionless
near the stove, his back bent, his eyes glaring at the floor,
turned suddenly around and set out towards the door swinging his shoulders. At the wooden door he looked back.

'I'm going to have my lunch,' he said ironically, twirling
his colourless moustache, 'but let me tell you, women, it's a
rotten world in which one is compelled to steal.'

The women picked up the thread he had dropped and fell
to imagining in a wealth of capricious detail the endless
variety of relationships between master and servant. They
stuck their sniffing, pointed noses into the gentry's full
larders, made an inventory of the never seen and yet pre-
cisely known stock, weighed the material and aesthetic difference between a thin soup and smoked gammon and then,
returning from the adventure with a melancholy, patriotic
sigh, began with strong hands and long-suffering souls to
translate the soup into reality. Meanwhile the widow Daniska
and Aunt Mari drew back into a corner and started a low
but excited conversation.

'Did you hear what he said?' asked Mrs. Daniska. 'He's compelled to steal! Do you think he is gone to the furnace room for coal?'

'It was around this time that I saw him coming out of it yesterday.'

'Sh . . . sh!' whispered the widow Daniska.

Aunt Mari turned her head and threw a quick glance at the old woman in mourning dozing in an armchair placed against the wall and her son sitting by her.

'Nothing to fear from them,' she said, 'they are Jews . . .'

'Jews?' Mrs. Daniska exclaimed in alarm. 'What did you say? . . . Jews?'

'They have some kind of American passport,' Aunt Mari informed her, 'that's why they haven't been deported yet. Do have a look in the furnace room, Mrs. Daniska!'

'What am I to tell him if he finds me there?' asked the old woman walking with heavy, anxious steps towards the door.

The widow of Dr. Karoly Veress, the old lady in mourning who spoke with a German accent, woke in her armchair at exactly five o'clock every morning. As it would have embarrassed her to wake her neighbours and as with her somewhat uncertain, eighty-year-old legs and eyes she dared not embark alone on the journey—these tiny, furtive adventures frightened her more than the bombing—she had to wait until the whole cellar woke around seven and her son, with a dripping candle in one hand and the old lady's three handbags, her shawl and umbrella in the other, accompanied her to the little wood-shed at the far end of the corridor where, among the sour-smelling oak logs, holding on with one hand to the wall, she could, with a low but angry rumbling, relax the morning tension of her organs.

'If you only knew what torture it is to wait so long,' she told her son every morning, words and intonation unchanged, while, carefully tapping the uneven flagstones of the corridor she strove eagerly but with great circumspection towards her goal, pushing forward her head wrapped in a thick white shawl, extending her left arm and tilting her body after it, a living example of passionate motion, its rhythm disciplined only by a lifetime of fateful experience.

The time between five and seven was usually spent in pondering those experiences. Fixing her tired eyes on the flickering oil lamp that hung on the opposite wall of the cellar—which, like the fire of a distant lighthouse, gave warning but no light—the old lady carefully scrutinized the diverse phases of her life. One by one, memories of mineral rigidity came to life dragging their giant, swaying shadow-bodies through the dark cellar which readily fell in with the wiles of the unreal and, like a revolving stage, took the rapidly changing scenes on its lap.

'If only I knew what time it is!' said the old lady now and again after one scene or another, whipping the floor with her cane whenever her body reminded her with a rude gesture of the passing of time. 'Are you going to sleep forever, apes?'

During the day as well there was plenty of time for the weighing of memories. As the inhabitants of the cellar (she had only known them for a week) drew away from her because of her San Salvador citizenship—her last living relative had sent that from Switzerland—and her son sat beside her in silence, his head bent. Mrs. Veress had sufficient leisure not only to revive her past but also to engage in a loftier occupation: she recited poetry, murmuring verses in a low voice, with wide-open, ecstatic eyes. Like the earth which catches and preserves its prehistory in its deeper layers while the changes taking place on its surface are blown away by the wind within hours, the old lady's memory retained the pliocene events of her life that had withstood every crisis petrified and unmarred. She carried with her towards her grave all that she had learned at the age of seventeen, poems by Goethe and Byron, entire scenes from Shakespeare's dramas, Klopstock's odes and Lessing's epigrams without a single gap, in all their full pomp, unaltered in form, like a collection of minerals; while she dusted away all recent events and often forgot that she was living in a strange house among strangers and that only a miracle had saved her from being shot dead.

'*Heraus in eure Schatten, rege Gipfel!*' she declaimed, sitting in her armchair at dawn when her bladder was giving her too much trouble, wagging her head, and throwing disapproving, indignant glances at her neighbours as they snored unsuspectingly, in cheerful unison under heavy blankets in the see-sawing, weak light of the oil lamp.

'Did you hear, Tamas, they say we are Jews!' she whispered to her son when the widow Daniska and Aunt Mari passed her armchair on their way to the landing. 'I wonder how they know?'

'Don't pay any attention to them, mother!' said her son.

'How could I not pay attention,' the old woman grumbled. 'Crazy as people are today, they may denounce us!'

Two strange men came in from the landing accompanied by the assistant janitor. For a few seconds they remained standing at the entrance, surveying the cellar, then walked straight to the old lady's armchair. One of the men lifted his hat.

'Mrs. Karoly Veress, widow?'

Her son rose.

'Yes, my mother.'

'Your mother,' the man repeated. 'Tamas Veress?'

'Yes, that is my name.'

'State police investigator,' the man said, 'take your papers and come with us.'

The old lady who had, in the meantime, begun her daily gymnastic exercises—she performed every day before breakfast 400 arm, wrist, leg, knee and ankle exercises in a pre-

cisely determined order and distribution—threw both her
arms up horizontally towards the detective.

'I am sorry,' she said, 'but I shall have to ask you to wait
because I cannot go now.' With a graceful gesture of her
hand she pointed to the nearby bed. 'Please, take a seat. I
shall be ready in half an hour and then I am at your disposal.'

'What?' the detective asked.

The old lady flung her arms up again.

'I am indeed sorry to have to ask you to wait, gentlemen,'
she said panting a little, 'but I cannot interrupt my exercises. True, they won't take long, but afterwards I shall have
to rest half an hour as I am usually a bit overheated from
the exertion. Now I must not speak.'

The women who had remained in the cellar had come to
stand round the small group. Tamas Veress who had, in the
meantime, drawn the other detective aside, had succeeded,
after a little bargaining, in getting permission to leave his
eighty-year-old mother—of whose escape there was little
danger—in the cellar, while he accompanied the detectives to
Police Headquarters. He was released an hour later after he
had presented their San Salvador citizenship papers, their
permit of residence in Hungary and the letter of the Swiss
consul which entitled them to live in a Christian house. He
did not go back home. Taking a roundabout way, so as to
make certain he was not followed, he entered a house in the
Istvan Tisza street.

He rang the door-bell of a studio apartment. He had to
ring five times.

'You are late,' said the man who opened the door.

Veress did not reply at once. He sat down on a kitchen
stool and opened his overcoat.

'Here are the papers,' he said. 'A birth certificate from
Nagyvárad, and one from Kolozsvár, two marriage certificates
from the same places, a Catholic certificate of baptism from

Nagybánya. Three Swedish safe conducts. Two and two is four, five, eight. All right?'

He buttoned his overcoat.

'I was almost caught,' he said hoarsely. 'They took me to police headquarters with these papers in my pocket. Fortunately, I wasn't searched.'

'Where did they get you?' the man asked.

'In the air-raid shelter.'

'You were denounced?'

'Yes.'

'In that case you had better move,' the man advised. 'The Arrow-cross boys might show up in the evening.'

'You know of a place?' Veress asked.

The man shook his head.

'And nothing in sight?'

'No.'

'Give me a cigarette!' Veress said. 'Couldn't we stay with you for one night?'

'Impossible,' the man growled. 'Nobody can come here.'

The young man rose and walked towards the door. When he reached it he turned back once more.

'I shouldn't like my mother to be shot and thrown into the Danube,' he said. 'Take her in for one night. I know you've had others sleeping here.'

The man shook his head again.

'Impossible,' he said, 'I am very sorry. Come back tomorrow or the day after in the late afternoon, perhaps I can find something by then.'

His wife, a grey-haired, fat woman with a pink complexion who had been kneading bread in a blue basin at the kitchen table during their conversation, suddenly turned back.

'What's the use of his coming here?' she said nervously. 'We can't find him a place anyway. If he had come two days earlier . . .'

'You're out of luck,' said the man yawning. He opened the door.

Dull explosions were heard from far away, like the noise of a distant pool-room. It was pouring with rain. By the time Veress reached home, the majority of the tenants had come down from the flats, the cellar was humming with lively talk. His mother was sitting in her armchair with her eyes closed. Her bony face with its carved chin and big, straight nose, was hard as an epitaph. Although she was a little deaf in both ears she recognised her son's steps from afar: her cheeks filled out suddenly, her eyes opened, grew larger, and sparkled.

'Well,' she said.

'Everything's all right, mother,' her son said. 'They wanted to see our papers. I had to wait for a long time, there were many before me.'

The old woman nodded.

'I thought so,' she said. 'It took a long time. Help me get up.'

'What for?'

'What for?' the old lady whispered angrily, 'I want to go out there again. I haven't been out there since seven o'clock this morning. How long, do you think, I can stand it? *Quo usque tandem abutere Catilina patientia nostra*, your father always used to say.'

On the way back they stopped at the staircase leading into the yard.

'I got rid of them quickly, didn't I?' she asked. 'I told them off, didn't I? Expecting me to go to Headquarters and present my papers. As if they couldn't have looked at those papers right here. They were scared of me, weren't they?'

'They certainly were, mother,' her son nodded.

The old lady burst out laughing.

'You should have seen his face!' she said while bringing

out her fine cambric handkerchief from the pocket of her
winter coat and wiping her lips. 'He stared at me in such a
way I was afraid he'd have a stroke. What I should have
really liked to do was to ask him: My good sir, don't you
know what physical culture is?'

The noise of planes penetrated from the yard.

'Air-raid?' the old lady asked. 'Good thing you are back.
If you hadn't come until two o'clock I'd have run after you.'

Tamas laughed.

'To Police Headquarters?'

'I have already arranged that with Aunt Mari, she was
going to accompany me,' the old lady informed him. 'We
shall wait until two, I told her when she sat down next to me
to comfort me, if he doesn't come by then, we shall go and
fetch him . . . Couldn't we go up to the yard for a little walk?'

'Not now, mother.'

The old lady's face turned suddenly poppy-red with fury.

'How much longer am I to wait!' she cried hitting the
stone floor with her stick. 'Yesterday you said that the Russians were already at the Eastern Railway Station. Twenty-
two years ago, in 1922, when we got back from Savanyukut
and there were neither street-cars nor taxis, old as I was, I
walked from the Eastern Station to Arpad street in three
quarters of an hour. These people have been on the way for
a whole day now . . .'

Above them, footsteps descended the stairs. The old lady
fell silent.

'Who is that coming?' she cried throwing back her head.
'The lawyer's wife?'

'In person, dear Mrs. Veress,' replied Mrs. Bor when she
reached the bottom of the stairs. Her husband, coming down
behind her, lifted his hat and walked on without a word.

'So here's your boy,' the woman said smiling; her huge,
red face with the pointed teeth in it, shone in the tired air

of the cellar as if a god had moulded it from the substance
of summer. 'Didn't I tell you, dear Mrs. Veress, that your son
was all right but he'd certainly got a long wait . . .'

She took the old lady's arm.

'Let's go in,' she said, 'there's an air-raid coming . . . So
they let you go at Headquarters, Mr. Veress . . .'

'As you see, Mrs. Bor.'

'They gave you back your papers, of course.'

The young man made no reply. He waited until his mother
had entered the shelter from the landing and advanced along
the narrow path between the beds with a loud tapping of
her stick.

'Just a moment,' he said to the lawyer's wife who was
about to follow her. 'Was it you who denounced us to the
police?'

The woman turned slowly round.

'What gives you that idea?' she asked calmly, but her face
turned a shade paler.

'The detective told me.'

'The detective lied,' the woman said. 'I did not denounce
you. I was at the police station and I asked them whether I
was allowed to keep foreign citizens in the house, but I did
not denounce you. I am block-warden, Mr. Veress, I have
my responsibilities.'

'Did you ask the Arrow-cross party as well?' the young
man asked.

'What do I care about the Arrow-cross party!' the woman
cried. The light of the storm-lamp illuminated her white
animal teeth, the black hair piled up on her head sparkled
with electricity. 'You know very well that I don't belong
to them!'

The young man nodded.

'I don't know it,' he said drily, 'but if you don't then it
is a pity you denounced us, Mrs. Bor. Because if someone from

the police puts the Arrow-cross people on us, then we won't be the only ones taken away from here tonight.'

The afternoon passed in relative calm, even the expected air-raid did not materialise. Rumour had it that the Germans were attempting a breakthrough in the Székesfehérvár area, and the Russians had obviously concentrated their air force in that region. The ordered schedule of the cellar disintegrated, hardly ten or fifteen people loitered in the two large rooms and even these were either sleeping or lying on their beds, their nerves relaxed. The women had scattered in the various flats and the majority of the men stood around in the yard smoking or looking out from the front-door at the devastated street and the fast darkening winter sky, the low clouds of which were, at times, illuminated by the flash of a distant gun. Now and again a fierce gust of wind would sweep the street from the direction of the Danube.

Mrs. Milos stood smoking in one of the recesses of the lobby, opposite the spiral stairs. When council secretary Finiasz, coming in from the yard, turned into the narrow corridor leading to the shelter, she threw away her cigarette.

In spite of the darkness she noticed that the council secretary was startled by her presence, and instead of stopping took another step towards the shelter. Only then did he turn back.

'Why are you spying on me?' he asked nervously.

The woman did not reply to the question.

'We go in the back way,' she said. 'I have to talk to you.'

'What is there to talk about!' the man growled. 'Talk . . . always talk . . .'

The small recesses opening on both sides of the corridor had been furnished by the more well-to-do tenants with divans, armchairs, curtains, as private sitting-rooms; Some had even put a stove in and spent their nights there. Mrs. Milos's private cellar was at the end of the corridor, next to

the furnace room. The council secretary stopped at the
door.

'I am not going in,' he said when he heard the woman rum-
maging among her keys.

She did not answer. The door opened with a creak.

'Didn't you hear me? I am not going in.'

'Are you afraid of me?' the woman asked.

The ceiling here was so low that the man bent his head
involuntarily so as not to hurt it in the dense darkness.

'What is the point in my going in?' the man murmured.
'If you only want to talk, we can talk here.'

He heard her striking a match inside.

'I want to see your face,' the woman said. The pale light
of the candle fell like a translucent, yellow veil on her slender,
supple neck and lent a brightness to the heavy, red lips protruding from her thin bird's face. Behind her back, a picture
of Christ hung on the board-wall in a yellow puddle of light.

'Come in, Lajos, don't be afraid of me,' the woman said.
With one smooth movement she stood before the council
secretary and put both arms around his neck. The man drew
back.

'Stop that!' he said irritably.

The woman immediately dropped her arms.

'Lajos, what have I done to you?' she whispered. Her eyes
filled with tears, her face turned grey like a deserted street.

'Is that all we have to worry about, damn it?' the man
swore, striking the thin board-wall with his fist. The dull
sound answered, as though in echo, by a thunderous explosion from the direction of the yard. The death-rattle of the
world above made the candle-flame flutter and the shadows
leapt about like wild goats in the narrow recess lined with
red carpets and curtains. The effects of the blast had not
yet settled when a new explosion whizzed along the corridor
shaking the walls.

'Were these hits?' asked the woman.

'What else?' the man replied ironically. Suppressed fury drove the blood to his head.

'Could you do me a favour and not throw yourself at me in front of my wife?' he growled pushing forward his mighty, square chin. 'Do you think people are blind? God damn it to hell, don't you have any shame left in you?'

'No,' replied the woman simply.

'Well, as far as I'm concerned, I've had enough!' the council secretary burst out with such anger that his knees began to shake. 'Enough, I say . . .'

'Of me?'

'Of you too.'

'Then why aren't you going?'

The man lowered his eyes, his lips twitched almost imperceptibly. For a few seconds he stood there, silent, then, lifting his hand in an uncertain movement to the back of his head he turned away slowly. But before he had finished turning the woman stepped up to him and took his arm.

'Lajos,' she said entreatingly, 'what have I done?'

'Nothing.'

'Calm yourself, I beg you!' The woman placed her cool hand on the man's neck.

The explosions now followed each other uninterruptedly, the narrow cubicle danced, trembling, on the sound waves. The picture of Christ, hanging near the edge of the red wall-carpet swung backwards and forwards in the blast which was throwing the furniture about—the red plush divan, the bow legged table and the two velvet chairs—as if it had suddenly sucked them clean of weight.

'You didn't do anything,' the council secretary said gnashing his teeth. 'You didn't pull up your skirt in front of my wife, did you? Only almost. Don't you understand? I've had enough of you!'

'Obviously you have other things to worry about,' the woman said enunciating every word clearly and emphatically.

'I beg your pardon?'

'You're afraid for your skin, aren't you?' She bent forward, her eyes contracted like those of a cat before it jumps, and she pressed both fists to her groin.

'Are you threatening me? Careful, you might burn your fingers!'

'You can still escape to Buda,' the woman whispered. 'Go on, get away, go over to Buda before it is too late. Very soon, we'll live in a world where anyone who has a single enemy should start digging his grave today!'

'Will you denounce me?'

The woman nodded without a word. The floor beneath their feet rose again, and dust blew in through the cracks in the door. Both sat down involuntarily on the red plush divan.

'Why not?' the woman said after a while dispassionately. 'You have ruined me, so why shouldn't I ruin you as well? They'll take away my flat...'

'How did I ruin you?'

'You don't love me!'

'Jesus Christ! Is this the time for loving?' the man had to shout to be heard above the successive explosions. The candle went out.

'The candle's gone out,' he said surprised, lowering his voice involuntarily. 'What do you want from me?'

The divan creaked.

'Lajos,' he heard the woman's voice in the dark. 'Why do we have to hurt each other?'

'Light the candle,' the council secretary said.

Instead of answering the woman drew closer and touched him with a lewd gesture. He drew back. For a moment there was silence.

'There you are!' the woman whispered, panting. 'I knew that you no longer loved me. And now go! I never want to see you again as long as I live!'

She waited until the pocket torch with its swinging beam of light had disappeared behind the turn in the corridor, then she locked the door and lay down on the divan. Council secretary Finiasz went straight to the air-raid shelter, which had, in the meantime, filled up again. The Bor couple were not yet in their place but his wife had already gone to bed and supervised the child's dinner. He had a large piece of bread and dripping, and a beautiful, red apple. Two beds away, a blond, skinny lad, brother of the assistant janitor's wife, was sitting with his back to the wall watching the listlessly eating child with bulging eyes. His lips moved in time with the lazy chewing. The council secretary sat down in the arm-chair.

'Where have you been?' his wife asked. 'What's the matter with you?' she added alarmed when she noticed that big drops of sweat covered the man's large, sanguine face, the corners of his nose, his forehead.

He glanced at the child and shook his head silently.

'You can speak,' the woman said in a low voice. 'He isn't listening.'

'I talked to her,' the council secretary said quickly.

'Well?'

'I broke with her.'

'For good?' the woman asked in a low voice, bending closer.

The man nodded. 'It's a pity, though,' he whispered. 'We were in too much of a hurry. She threatened me.'

'What with?'

'She said she'd denounce me. I won't get away with it. You could have waited a little longer.'

The tiny, mouse-faced woman picked up the plate lying

on her lap with a big piece of bread and dripping on it, and
flung it with all her strength to the floor. The fragments
scattered wide on the cement floor and the child, lying next
to her, winced as if she had slapped him.

'What's going on here, are you bombing us too?' said
Mrs. Bor who had just reached the bed with a loaded tray
in her hand. 'Keep cool, children, here's your dinner! Lajos,
would you take the tea pot off the tray?'

'Where did you make the tea?' the man asked.

'At the assistant janitor's. They're having a fine old time
up there, my children,' she reported while putting down the
tray on the bed and placing plates around it. Her round face
under the wealth of piled-up black hair bent over the golden-
yellow silk counterpane like Ceres's face once upon a time
when she inspected the rich wheat fields of Greece. 'Half a
dozen armed Arrow-cross men are sitting in the kitchen,
bottles of wine are lined up on the table, and on the floor,
at their feet, stands a huge laundry basket full of silk shirts,
new shoes, damask table-cloths and God knows what else. I
saw two gold watches on the table.'

'They won't enjoy it for much longer,' the council secretary said.

'Quite possibly,' said the woman curtly. 'By the way, did
you know that the police let the Jew go?'

'Good for them!' cried Mrs. Finiasz so loudly that some
of her neighbours turned round questioningly.

The lawyer's wife sat down on a foot-stool between the
two beds and poured out the tea.

'How I've begged Karoly,' she said quietly, 'to move to
Buda to my mother's villa. In a week people will hang here
side by side like sausages in the loft.'

'We too?' asked Mrs. Finiasz throwing a quick glance at
her husband.

'We too.'

'Where will we hang, mummy?' asked the child who had, in the meantime, finished his beautiful red apple and thrown the core at the head of the assistant-janitor's brother-in-law. The lad wiped his face with the back of his hand and turned away. In the corner, the widow Daniska and Aunt Mari squatted on two kitchen chairs weaving the black cloth of their shared troubles with burning cheeks and excited whispers.

'Did you know that the assistant-janitor is entertaining Arrow-cross men?' the widow Daniska asked.

'I've just come from there,' the bootmaker's widow said. 'I've even spoken to them.'

'What do they say?'

'They are crazy!' Aunt Mari replied, frightened. 'They've brought a laundry basket full of gold, diamonds, boots and now their sharing them. And the assistant-janitor is standing there watching them coldly, and he says he doesn't want any of it because they'll have to give it all back, anyway.'

'Give it back?' the widow Daniska asked, scared.

'Sure!' Aunt Mari nodded and the spectacles inherited from her husband flashed severely in the soft light of the candle. 'Haven't you heard that Mrs. Milos will have to give back the flat?'

The old laundress made no reply.

'Now they're sharing the loot and at night they'll go raiding,' the bootmaker's widow went on. 'To taste blood, before they're all hanged, they say. Have they all gone mad?'

'Before they're all hanged?' the widow Daniska repeated.

Aunt Mari nodded.

'Look! What is the matter with Mr. Finiasz?' she said pushing her spectacles up her nose and inspecting the council secretary sitting three beds away. 'Look! His teeth are chattering and he is as pale as death!'

'His forehead is covered in sweat,' the widow Daniska stated.

'He must be ill,' Aunt Mari opined. She threw another glance at the council secretary who sat with his head lowered, a small tea cup in his hand, motionless, staring at the floor, then she jumped up from her chair. 'I'm going out to the back,' she whispered, 'to send the lad away. They might start their raiding right here!'

'God help me!' the widow Daniska whispered back.

'What's the matter?'

'I'm coming with you,' the old laundress said getting off her chair.

They set out one behind the other along the narrow path between the beds that led through the board-door and the other cellar toward the lobby. Most of the cellar-dwellers were already in bed, some of them asleep. In the second cellar, opposite the exit, in a cubicle between two pillars that was illuminated by a separate candle which closed itself in, with-holding even its light, a few men were playing cards, their purple faces bent over the table.

'God help me!' the widow Daniska whispered again when they reached the cold lobby.

'What's the matter with you?'

The night was clear, silent. From the darkness of the sky pouring down over the spiral stairs and circulating in the deeper darkness below as blood circulates in the body, a spark of hope would flash at times into this dim underworld. The two old women stopped and stared silently for a moment. They heard a hoarse, drunken yell from above, a revolver shot, singing.

The widow Daniska extricated a small parcel from her voluminous bosom and with trembling fingers, undid the tissue paper. It contained a small silver cross without a chain.

'Aunt Mari, do I have to give this back?' the old woman

asked and her eyes filled with tears. 'I found it last night on the stair-case but I know whose it is.'

'If you know then give it back,' Aunt Mari said. 'The devil take this miserable world!'

The two widows set out together toward the furnace room. As they had no lamp, they advanced in the blind darkness cautiously, with hands groping on the wall, and seeking feet, and they struck a match only when, after the second turning they had to find the board-door of the furnace room. The deserter lay in the corner, behind a pile of coal, his legs wide-spread, his cheek on the ground.

For a while they called him in vain, he didn't wake up. Aunt Mari squatted down next to him, shook his shoulder, pinched his ear, spoke to him in desperate whispers, but the lad was so deeply asleep that he didn't even raise his hand to protest. And when, finally, both widows went to work on him and, joining forces, turned him over on his back, he opened his eyes for a brief second.

'Get up, child,' the widow Daniska whispered in his ear, 'you must go, there are Arrow-cross men in the building!'

'Where?' asked the lad and closed his eyes to shut out the light of the match that cut like a knife.

'In the house!' Mrs. Daniska whispered.

'In the house,' the young man repeated after her. He sat up, shook his head, lay back again. No warning, no argument could induce him to continue the conversation, even less to rise and leave that ill-omened place. The moment Aunt Mari stopped shaking his shoulder he immediately began to snore.

After a while the two widows gave up the vain attempt and, in astounded silence, left the furnace room. The sleeper, however, was awakened by the very silence. When they reached the board-door a few pieces of coal came rolling down noisily as if someone had directed an angry kick at the pile.

'I'm not going,' they heard a hoarse voice behind them in the darkness. 'Not even if I have to rot here!'

'God help you, child, get a hold on yourself!' said Aunt Mari, frightened. But they got no reply. Old Mrs. Daniska's knees shook so that she had to be supported and when they got back to the lobby she flopped down on the lowest step of the spiral stairs, regardless of the ice-cold, misty air blowing in from the yard. Snatches of drunken singing could be heard from the assistant janitor's flat.

In the cellar the people had retired to bed. The majority were lying down fully clothed; some hadn't even taken their shoes off; raised on one elbow they gazed into the dull semi-obscurity, or, pulled their hats over their eyes to protect themselves against the blinding light of awareness. There was hardly any conversation going on. At moments the silence was so complete that one could discern the chattering of council secretary Finiasz's teeth. Soft moans rose here and there but only a fourteen year old girl who had recently lost her father in an air-raid, had the courage to cry aloud.

About eight o'clock the assistant janitor had been down in the cellar. He had stayed only a few minutes, pretended that he was looking for something among his belongings, and had put a small iron pan under his arm.

'There'll be a raid soon,' he remarked offhandedly. 'You'd better get your papers ready.'

He repeated the warning in the second cellar as well, looking pointedly at Tamas Veress and his mother who were sitting quietly in their usual place.

'Come here, man, come here!' the old lady called to him raising her head alertly on the look-out for an entertaining conversation. 'Come here! What were you winking for?'

'I didn't wink,' said the assistant janitor, stopping for a moment by the old lady's chair. 'I was only looking to see whether you were asleep.'

'But you also said something,' the old lady insisted. 'What did you say?'

There came no reply.

'You must forgive me, my good man,' the old lady excused herself with a charming smile, 'but I am hard of hearing, and like most deaf people, apt to imagine things. I thought you had said something. Well, then, God bless you, my good man, have a good rest tonight, you need it.'

She smiled, nodded, the assistant janitor raised his hat and left. The women pulled their handbags closer, the men patted their wallets. The widow Daniska felt that the last of her strength was seeping out of her, she lay down flat on her bed and closed her eyes. Outside the night was calm, the besiegers were quiet, not a single shot went off, so everyone could wrap themselves in their own silence which let them straight down to hell on the silk thread of imagination. The darkness was unbearable. Mrs. Bor rose and lit another candle. Even through the closed cellar door they could hear the drunken shouting and revolver shots coming from the yard.

Aunt Mari picked up her little foot-stool and went out into the lobby. No one asked her where she was going. She put the foot-stool down next to the spiral stairs, sat down, folded her hands in her lap and began her vigil. After a while, young Veress joined her. He lit a cigarette but stayed out there even after it was smoked. Outside, a dense fog must have descended on the town because the spiral staircase seemed to be wrapped in steam and even the singing, overflowing from the assistant janitor's flat, sounded duller.

Aunt Mari's watchful eyes followed the young man as he walked with long strides up and down the lobby.

'Why aren't you running away, young man?' she asked when, deep in thought, Tamas stopped near her.

'I am not going to leave my mother.'

The old woman hummed.

'And why don't you take the old lady as well?'

'The front door is locked,' Veress replied. 'Besides, my mother wouldn't be able to take ten steps in this darkness.'

They fell silent. Up in the yard a door was flung open, a medley of thick voices streamed out and was cut off suddenly by another banging of the door. The noise of uncertain, heavy steps sounded from the yard.

'He is alone,' the old woman said. 'Taking the air.'

Veress listened without a word.

'Why don't you hide in one of the flats?' Aunt Mari asked. 'If I had one, I'd give you the key. But there must be someone . . .'

'There isn't,' Veress said.

'Have you tried?'

'I have.'

'Try again,' the old woman advised. 'If they catch you when they are in a bad mood they'll take you down to the Danube and shoot both of you. In the house where I lived they caught a deserter, his mother was shot dead, same as him. Where have you tried?'

Veress did not reply, at once.

'I tried council secretary Finiasz,' he said after a while. 'He is coming towards the cellar stairs, can you hear him?'

'There's nothing to fear as long as he's alone,' the old woman mumbled.

The steps, splashing in snow-water, were now more clearly discernible; they stopped, then started again. A moment later they stopped for good near the cellar stairs. Thick, retching sounds were heard, then disjointed garglings. Aunt Mari laughed softly.

'He's vomiting,' she whispered. 'The pig! Isn't he ashamed of himself!'

'And this pig will shoot me,' said Veress.

The bootmaker's widow shook her head.

'Being drunk is not a crime,' she said quietly. 'Everyone has a right to some fun even if someone else has to pay the price. Why did the gentry drag the poor people into this war? That's where they learned to kill.'

Veress made no reply. The cellar door creaked open, the teenage brother of the assistant janitor's wife stuck out his head and addressed the young man.

'The old lady is asking for you,' he said with lowered eyes. 'Go in, sir, I'll stay out here until you return.'

Old Mrs. Veress was sitting bolt upright in her armchair, resting her hand on the knob of her stick. Her two patent-leather bags stood on the floor at her feet, her umbrella hung from the back of the chair, her head, wrapped in her black lace shawl, was supported by a tiny, pale-green silk cushion. 'I am glad you are here,' she said when she heard her son's steps and she tapped the floor twice with her stick.

'You wish to go out to the back, mother?' the young man asked.

The old lady shrugged irritably.

'Do you think that's all I ever want you for?' she grumbled. 'Sit down by me. I hear that there are Arrow-cross men in the house.'

'Yes, mother, but they are here as guests.'

'Fine,' the old lady said. 'Everyone here is expecting a raid. Take the money, your father's gold watch and ring, from my patent leather bag and try to get out of the building. I hear the front door is locked. Give the gold watch to the janitor if he lets you out. If he doesn't, try to get out through the pub or by a window in a ground floor flat.'

'I wouldn't even think of it.'

The old lady's face turned suddenly white, then, without transition, blood-red, under the double pressure of love and anger.

'Don't argue!' she shouted, hitting the floor furiously with her stick. 'What help is it to me if you get shot too! And if they leave us alone, we meet here tomorrow morning. Off you go!'

The young man burst out laughing.

'Don't shout, mother, as if you were alone,' he said catching the old lady's peremptory index finger in his hand with a pacifying gesture. 'Everyone is asleep.'

'Nobody is asleep,' the old lady said. 'Half of them are afraid of the Arrow-cross people, the other half of the Russians. I've been hearing for two days that they are at the Eastern Station. They certainly are a lazy crowd, even I would have got here by this time. Now, as I said, off you go!'

Before her son could answer, she rose from her armchair, put both arms round the young man's neck, gave his bottom an affectionate pat with her stick and kissed him passionately on the mouth with her wrinkled lips.

'God be with you,' she murmured. 'We may never see each other again.'

At that moment the noise of movement, frightened exclamations, were heard from the next cellar. The connecting door flew open and the brother of the assistant janitor's wife jumped into the vibrating light of the night-lamp, his thin neck tensing forward, his two arms raised.

'They are coming!' he cried.

'I don't know what to do,' Mrs. Bor whispered to her husband and her large, healthy face turned ashy grey under the thick, black crown of hair. They had to decide at once, she told her husband. He lit a cigarette in his excitement although smoking was prohibited in the cellar; however, in the general pandemonium, no one noticed. The whole cellar was humming with excitement, but the emotion was cold, not daring to show itself, it turned in on itself. Everyone pretended indifference. Latent in each slow, sluggish movement, was the speed of a fleeing fawn. Those who were lying down

got up and put on their shoes, those who had been sitting
up lay down again as if, by changing their position, they
could change their dangerous situation. Body and soul were
so completely attuned that—when emotion changed its
rhythm—feet, hands, eyelashes and the pores of the skin
immediately adjusted themselves to it, concealing the inner
upheaval; no one was misled by another's apparent indifference; on the contrary, it quickened one's sensibilities.

In a corner someone blew out a candle to make it darker,
and at the same moment, in another corner someone lit another candle, to make it lighter. There were a good many
families in the house who were members of the Arrow-cross
party, or at least sympathised with it, but now they were
just as fidgety as their neutral fellows or those few stubborn
burghers who dug their heels in and opposed the stream,
perhaps neither in word nor in deed, but out of fastidiousness.
At a glance one could hardly notice the difference between
the various layers. The lawyer Bor and his wife had, for
long, been members of the Arrow-cross Party, but they were
as pale as Tamas Veress, the citizen of San Salvador. They
were balanced on the razor's edge. The woman was block-
warden, it was part of her job to know that tropical citizen-
ships always covered Jews and she should have reported it to
the Party long ago; if she did not warn these raiding Arrow-
cross men now, they might well bring her to book for hiding
Jews. In addition, the approaching company was dead drunk
—their confused shouting could already be heard from the
lobby and then who knew what shape that calling to account
would take. If, on the other hand, she did tell them, a thing
that could hardly be kept secret, and Veress and his mother
were as a result taken away and executed, in a week's time,
when the Russians arrived, she would be denounced and the
journey to the scaffold or lamp-post would not be any longer
than the Jews' journey from Nador Street to the Danube.

'How I begged you to move to Buda, to my mother's!' she said to her husband who sat staring in front of him, chewing his moustache, his face chalk-white.

'It won't take a week . . . they'll be here in three days!' whispered council secretary Finiasz who was sitting in a green leather armchair opposite, pressing a white silk handkerchief to his mouth to stop the intolerable chattering of his teeth. The lawyer's wife threw him a hate-filled glance.

'Now, what's the matter with you?' she said contemptuously. 'How can someone who calls himself a man be such a coward?'

'You shut your trap!' the council secretary growled. 'Mind your own business'

Outside it had begun to rain. Through the ventilator which was left open, they could hear the monotonous, gentle drumming of the rain-drops that, like an old song from an old, half-forgotten age, smuggled into the cellar the merciful memories of free winter nights. A sudden gust of wind swept the smell of snow as well into the faded air of the cellar which, revived, began to whirl. Mrs. Milos, who had returned to the shelter half an hour before, got up from her bed, stepped to the wall, re-arranged the holy picture that had swung to one side during the morning's air-raid, then sat back silently on her bed, directing her dim, rigid glance at the face of the council secretary sitting opposite her.

In the meantime the noise from the lobby had quietened down, the Arrow-cross men were obviously searching the private cellars along the corridor. The widow Daniska and Aunt Mari squatted trembling on the edge of their bed. The bootmaker's widow was so nervous that she took her spectacles off and hid them under her pillow. Mrs. Daniska was sweating with fear to such an extent that the cold perspiration had dried on to her skin and her entire body was itching.

It was evident that if the Arrow-cross men searched the whole cellar they would inevitably find the deserter concealed in the furnace room. Time passed slowly; it spread before them like the infinite, shoreless sea before a shipwreck; when the heightened moment lifted them up like the back of a wave, even from up there they could see only the thunderous desert of time reaching to the edge of the horizon. In people's souls fear grew in geometrical progression. Man is conscious of time only when there is too little or too much of it, that is, when it increases beyond bounds or suddenly runs out; on such occasions, its place is imperceptibly taken by another medium: anxiety, in whose stream the soul loses its sense of proportion, its sense of direction, its everyday weight, and founders in it as helplessly as a body falling unexpectedly from the air into the mud of a swamp, or the water of a river. To Mrs. Daniska it seemed as if she had been waiting for the entrance of the Arrow-cross men, not ten minutes but ten days, and as every coming minute would use up at least one full day of her life force, her vitality, it can be said that she was living not in time but in fear, and that time only exists when it doesn't exist.

Not even ten minutes had gone by since the Arrow-cross men had left the lobby when quick, hard steps were heard in the oppressive silence, from the direction of the second cellar, the door flew open, and the deserter appeared in the lamplight. His clothes glistened black from the coal-dust, his face and hands were also besmeared with it. In a second his eyes had found the two petrified old women and immediately he set out towards them. The noise made by the Arrow-cross men had awakened him in time and he had fled along the other branch of the corridor. He hoped that the air-raid shelter itself had already weathered the raid and he could hide there until the Arrow-cross men had left the house. As soon as he learned from Aunt Mari that they had not been in the shelter yet, he turned around and left the cellar at a run. The two old women hadn't had time to recover from their fright nor had Mrs. Bor, busy with her own troubles, been able to ask what this stranger was doing in the house in the middle of the night, when the now familiar quick, hard steps were heard again and the deserter appeared again in the door. His teeth sparkled crystal white in his blackened face and his eyes shone glassily with fright. The front door was locked, he couldn't get out of the house. The key was in the pocket of the janitor who, together with the assistant janitor, was trailing along with the Arrow-cross boys. Without finishing his sentence, the fugitive turned his back on the two old women and ran out of the cellar.

The figure of a fleeing man will, in a second, grow to such proportions from the weight of his emotions that, before our very eyes, he sheds the ordinary measurements of man and enters the mirror of our senses as a towering giant. His feet, hands, features and movements run through us multiplied manifold and leave giant foot-prints in the soft soil of memory. Fear transforms not only time at its own pleasure, but also space; the running figure of the deserter—although the time for observation was short—penetrated through the nervous systems of the people with as much emotional weight as if a Titan had run out of the cellar in front of their eyes. His coal-dusty suit, white teeth, wet, blond hair, and long, waving arms created, in a second, as many involved and definite memories as if they had watched him for hours. They all recognised themselves in the fleeing figure and paled under the confrontation.

Council secretary Finiasz jumped up from his armchair and started, involuntarily, towards the door. Someone moaned loudly and in a corner an old woman clapped her hands together and began to wail. Mrs. Milos bent forward and put her hand on the arm of the council secretary.

'Stay,' she said in a loud voice.

A new wave of noise washed in through the door. A thick voice, surrounded by a spray of thin voices, and behind them a formless, monotonous humming. In the next cellar some-one overturned a chair.

'Where are the two Veresses?' Mrs. Milos asked.

Silence fell in the low room, one could hear the sibilant sputtering of the candle.

'Where have the Jews gone to?' Mrs. Milos repeated.

Everyone turned round; the old lady's armchair and the white kitchen chair next to it, were empty.

'What Jews?' asked Mrs. Bor.

'Don't pretend,' cried Mrs. Milos and her slender neck above the fur coat flushed.

'I saw them here a moment ago,' said the lawyer.

'You know as well as I that they are Jews,' cried Mrs. Milos turning to the lawyer's wife. The latter made no reply. The noise seeping in from the lobby became more stratified, more involved, shouts, even snatches of words, could be dis-tinguished. Mrs. Milos rose and stepped before the council secretary.

'Did you hide them?' she asked in a loud voice.

'What is she saying?' a surprised, thick voice asked in the corner. 'Did she say he hid them?'

The council secretary stood motionless beside a bed his right hand pressing the silk handkerchief to his lips.

'Where did you hide them?'

'Calm down, Ilonka,' Dr. Bor said irritably. 'What has got into you?'

'What has got into me? I'll tell you. He is providing him-self with an alibi so's they shan't hang him next week.'

The council secretary still didn't answer. The lawyer's wife rose and stepped beside Mrs. Milos.

'He won't get away with that!' Mrs. Milos said in a low

voice but with such suppressed emotion that every breath she took could be clearly heard even in the farthest corner of the cellar.

The lawyer's wife took hold of her arm.

'Have you gone out of your mind?'

'Why don't you say something!' Dr. Bor said to the council secretary. 'They'll be here in a moment!'

'Sure, they'll be here in a moment!' Mrs. Milos's lustre-less eyes gleamed triumphantly. 'So where did you hide them?'

It grew a shade darker in the cellar; one of the candles had burnt itself out, the wick bent, the flame died. Pressing her two hands to her hips, Mrs. Milos bent forward and her rigid glance rested on the council secretary's face. 'Either you bring them back,' she said with the shadow of the dead candle in her voice, 'or I'll report you to the Arrow-cross for hiding Jews!'

'You're mad!' the lawyer's wife screamed. 'You want them to kill me too?'

The council secretary reached into his pocket, brought out a revolver and fired two bullets into the heart of the woman standing in front of him. Mrs. Milos collapsed without a sound and stretched out on the ground. A few minutes later, when they had lifted her on the bed and the first-aid nurse established that she was dead, old Mrs. Veress appeared in the connecting door leaning with one hand on her stick, the other on her son's arm. The women standing around the bed blocked her view of the body.

'Where have you been?' asked Mrs. Bor, her face ashen.

Old Mrs. Veress sat down in her armchair with a little groan, hung her stick on the arm of the chair and pulled her new Scottish plaid onto her knees.

'Out to the back,' she said jerking her head towards the wood-cellars. '*Naturalia non sunt turpia*, don't you know,' she added smiling. 'Besides, I did not wish to cause my son trouble in the middle of the raid.'

'You were in the lavatory?' the lawyer's wife asked pressing both hands on her stomach.

Old Mrs. Veress, who did not hear the question, wiped her forehead and lips with a tiny black lace handkerchief.

'By the way, the Arrow-cross men have gone,' she informed them. 'When we reached the lobby on our way back they were all hurrying towards the stairs. I can easily do without their company,' she added tactfully, 'for they were rather intoxicated.'

*   *   *

Learning that the Germans were evacuating Budapest and were going to blow up the bridges in an hour, the Arrow-cross men fled from the house in a panic. By the time Dr. Bor reached the top of the spiral stairs, there was not a soul in sight. The assistant-janitor's windows were dark, the street-door stood wide open. A few steps from the street-door, on the corner of the street leading to the Danube, a man stood in the middle of the road in his jacket, his head uncovered, staring motionless towards the Buda mountains.

'Is that you, janitor?' the lawyer asked when he reached him.

The man turned his head towards him. In the dense winter night the white of his eyes winked like a marsh-fire. In the great silence one could hear the chattering of his teeth.

'What a bloody cold wind!' he said.

'Where is your assistant?' the lawyer asked.

'Gone with them.'

For a while both kept silent.

'Good for him,' the lawyer said. 'He has no children.'

The janitor turned the whites of his eyes towards the lawyer.

'Good for him,' he repeated slowly. 'For if he hadn't gone I'd have kicked that Arrow-cross bastard out of here so fast...'

The lawyer did not immediately grasp the other's meaning. Involuntarily he lifted his hand but fortunately the movement merged with the darkness. He had to watch his breathing as well, it was liable to rasp in his excitement. A cold wind blew from the Danube, he began to shiver.

'I'm glad we got rid of him at last,' said the man next to him with ponderous, peasant calm. But his teeth continued to chatter. The sound of a rifle-shot reached them from the direction of Buda like a greeting from afar. 'Those who have something to fear did well to go, isn't it so, Dr. Bor?'

Below, in the shelter, all were sitting on their beds, fully dressed in the wavering shadow-cages thrown by two rows of pillars. The door to the lobby was wide open and this time a candle was burning in the lobby as well. At the foot of one of the beds an old woman prayed on her knees, her head bent; her two black shoes, standing on their toes, could be seen under her skirt, tapping rhythmically on the floor.

Dr. Bor sat down on the bed next to his wife.

'Is it true?' the woman asked.

'Yes.'

'Did you go outside?'

'To the corner.'

The lawyer glanced at the next bed with Mrs. Milos's sheet-covered body lying on it. The toes of her shoes and, at the other end, her nose, protruded sharply from the sheet.

'The janitor has already changed over,' he said ironically and his teeth began to chatter again. 'He has a quicker mind than I have. He almost got me.'

The woman turned her large, pale face towards him questioningly. Her thick, dark brows met above her nose and her white teeth seemed to have concentrated all the light in her mouth.

'He was cursing the Arrow-cross,' said the lawyer, wrinkling his nose.

His wife clapped her hands over her mouth.

'But he is a party member!'

'Perhaps only his son,' the man replied hoarsely. 'And he has run away.'

'Look!' whispered the woman, jerking her head in the direction of the opposite corner.

In the entire cellar only one person was asleep: Mrs. Karoly Veress. Resting her wrapped-up head on the green silk travelling cushion, she was breathing softly in the oblique candle-light; her straight, sharp-edged nose threw a small rectangular shadow on her left cheek. One of her hands lay on the shoulder of her son who was eating a slice of bread at her feet.

'His appetite's come back,' the lawyer said through chattering teeth.

The bridges were blown up after midnight. Council secretary Finiasz, who had been sitting beside his wife with his head lowered, his arms hanging, without a word, came suddenly to life.

'What was that?' he asked raising his head.

'They have blown up the bridges!' cried the lawyer at the top of his voice. His large, pale face flushed blood-red with fury and malice.

The door of the lobby flew open and shut with a bang.

'We're finished,' said the council secretary. He rose from his chair, then quickly sat down again.

'The Russians'll be here by morning,' cried the lawyer's wife hitting the bed with her fist. 'We shall be free again, Mr. Council Secretary!'

The explosions came rolling down into the cellar in uninterrupted succession, crushed the fluttering candle light and absorbed every latent sound. The door of the lobby flew open.

'Free again,' repeated the council secretary in a soundless moment between two explosions. He gave the woman a long-curious glance. 'I see,' he said. 'I understand, dear comrade.'

The deserter, who had come back to the cellar after the departure of the Arrow-cross and who was now lying on the widow Daniska's bed turned to Aunt Mari. 'What did she say about the Russians?' he asked.

The two widows were sitting on the edge of the bed, each watching the other's anxious face.

'They'll be here by morning, child,' Aunt Mari informed him.

'Of course they will,' said the lad. 'What time is it?'

'It must be after midnight,' the widow Daniska opined.

'Daybreak cannot be very far,' said Aunt Mari musingly.

The deserter shook his head laughing. With the two large coal-dust patches on his cheekbones, his black-pointed nose and russet hair he looked like a black painted clown in the court of the underworld.

'You whisper like bushes in the breeze,' he said. 'One cannot get a straight word out of you. Perhaps midnight . . . perhaps dawn . . . I asked you what time it was!'

'We don't know, child,' said Aunt Mari.

'Don't know . . . don't know . . .' grumbled the lad. 'It doesn't matter. I'm going back into the coal. For now its the Russians who will arrest me, isn't it so, auntie?'

'Is that what you are afraid of?' asked Aunt Mari.

The widow Daniska folded her hands in prayer and stared before her with tear-filled eyes. The explosions had ceased and the silence, like a wall above the river, had cut the town in two.

'You can see for yourself,' the lad said, 'that this will never end. Now they'll shoot at us from the other side. Now from one side, now from the other. Wherever you run, they shoot at you.'

The two widows remained silent. Aunt Mari twiddled her fingers.

'That's how it is in the world,' she said severely after a while. 'The poor man is always there where there's shooting. He's only got himself to blame, why doesn't he change it.'

'We'll change it, never fear,' murmured the young man. 'Is it certain that my mother is dead?'

The two old women nodded.

'They shot her twice?'

'Twice.'

'Then I heard right,' said the lad. 'I heard two shots, almost simultaneously. I thought they were firing after me. Both shots were for her?'

'Both.'

'Of course,' the young man murmured. 'Did it take her long to die?'

'An hour.'

The deserter rose and stretched.

'Let me have a piece of bread, I'm going back into the coal,' he said. He smoothed down his tousled, fair hair and pulled up his trousers. 'For once one begins to shoot,' he said moodily, 'one never stops as long as one lives.'

It was getting light when the first Russian soldier appeared in the cellar. His fur cap sat obliquely on his head and he held his machine-gun in his arms as if it were a baby. Although they lighted several candles in his honour, one could not distinguish his features under the soot and filth. His eyes wandered slowly round the cellar.

'Germanski?' he asked in a deep, throaty voice.

He had laughing, blue eyes. He walked round the cellar in

his soundless boots and gazed into every face. He stopped
before a little boy of six with an army cap on his head. He
said something in Russian which no one understood. For a
while he gazed at the child shaking his head, then, with two
fingers, he carefully lifted the cap from his head and flung
it into a corner. He laughed at the child, looked round once
more, then, with soundless steps, he ran from the cellar.

'Strike me dead!' cried Aunt Mari, swearing for the first
time in her entire life, and big tears of joy ran down her
cheeks from under the spectacles inherited from her husband.
'The war is over, so help me, Jesus! The war is over, to hell
with whoever invented it!'

'Come and have some breakfast, God damn it!' said the
widow Daniska with tears in her eyes, 'I'm starving, the devil
take this miserable world!' She took Aunt Mari's arm and
dragged her towards the shelf on which the cellar-dwellers
stored their food. 'Where's that bloody foot-stool?' she
grumbled. 'Hold me, Aunt Mari, I'm afraid I'll trip, to hell
with this blessed foot of mine!'

'I'm holding you,' shouted Aunt Mari, 'goddamn my weak
hands!'

The widow hopped onto the foot-stool like a grasshopper.
'I can't see my basket,' she murmured and wiped her eyes,
'the devil take whoever invented darkness!'

'What are you looking for, blast it!' said Aunt Mari. 'Tell
me!'

The widow Daniska climbed off the foot-stool with a basket
in her hand. 'I've got a little bread and honey left,' she said.
'Let's finish it before it goes to the dogs!'

THE PORTUGUESE PRINCESS

THE PORTUGUESE PRINCESS

ONE hour after the German evacuation, in the lowland village of B., on a hot summer day that tenderly wrapped and steeped in its brightness the big peasant houses of the quiet side street, one of the green-painted gates burst open suddenly and a boy of ten or twelve flew out of it in a wide arc. He turned two somersaults in the air, then lay stretched out on the ground with wide-spread arms. Behind him, the green-painted gate swung slowly to, its hinges squeaking cheerfully.

By the time the tiny clouds of dust had settled around the small body lying on the ground and the young acacia tree it had hit tilted back to its original graceful position, a fair-haired little girl had scrambled out of the roadside ditch, walked up to the sprawling boy and squatted down by his head.

'They kicked you out?'

The boy made no reply.

'So they kicked you out,' the little girl repeated wagging her head.

The boy lifted his hand above his face and in the precipitous sunshine examined his small, dirty fingers one by one.

'You noticed?' he murmured.

'You nearly uprooted that tree,' said the little girl looking at the acacia tree; its feathery shadows were still vibrating on the shimmering dust-carpet of the street.

'Why did they kick you out? Did you pinch something?'

'Shut up!' the boy growled.

For a moment the little girl gazed silently in front of her, then she lifted her hand and slapped the boy quickly. Then, like a little frog, she jumped away. After two or three jumps she stopped and, her head tilted, glanced back curiously. The boy hadn't moved.

'You can add that to the others, you worm!' the little girl said. 'And next time you are cheeky I'll stamp on you like an old shoe. You aren't worth a rotten fig! You don't get on with the peasants, you are kicked out of every house, and you are cheeky into the bargain.'

The boy sat up, beat the dust from his long, black hair with his palm, then suddenly, he burst into tears.

'You've got a dirtier mouth than my mother and she was bad enough,' he sniffed, wiping away his tears. 'A lot of comfort you are—all you can do is scold.'

'Shut your trap!' the little girl said.

The boy got to his knees and explored his back and hipbones with both hands.

'You don't even ask me if I'm hurt,' he said plaintively.

The little girl rose from her squatting position—they were of the same height—and looked him up and down contemptuously.

'Who cares?' she said curtly. 'I jumped out of a first-floor window once and nothing happened except that I limped for a week. There's nothing to whine about. Little worms like us don't get hurt. Wait till we grow up.'

Another tiny, fair head rose from the ditch.

'Can I come out?' the third child asked.

He seemed somewhat shorter than the other two and a year or two younger, but his face was clean as if a woman's hand had washed it.

'Shall I bring the luggage?' he asked.

The little girl turned to him immediately, her thin, freckled

face with the two precocious, flashing dark eyes suddenly
softened and filled with a rush of tenderness. In a second,
as if the wind had blown her there, she stood beside the
ditch.

'Are you hungry, Johnny?' she asked.

'Not very hungry yet,' the small boy replied.

The little girl wiped the child's nose with her skirt.

'Then leave the luggage where it is, we'll try another house
or two.'

'Shall I go?' Johnny asked.

'Certainly not!' the little girl said. 'That dog-catcher hasn't
earned a bean today.' She bent to the ear of the small boy.
'Cross my heart, I wouldn't mind if they caught him,' she
whispered her forehead turning suddenly red, 'he hasn't got
any more sense than a plate of tripe. Look at him brushing his
hair!'

The unpaved, dusty street ran between two rows of bushy-
topped acacia trees which, bending close, like the two blades
of a pair of scissors, caught between them the brilliant sum-
mery horizon. There wasn't a soul on the pavements, nor a
cart in the road, not a single hen scratched about along the
fences. When, at times, a lazy little breeze flitted among the
trees it caused such a cloud of dust that it lingered for the
next hour. The arid heat swallowed up every sound, even the
tiny crackle of the cow-dung drying in the middle of the road.
There was so little shadow left in the street that it would
have found room under the wing of a sparrow.

'Johnny, let's go on,' the little girl said, jumping with her
two quick, bare feet into the ditch. 'This street is no good, it
isn't worth a horse dropping. Peter!' she called out to the
dark, long-haired boy who stood leaning his back against the
acacia tree and staring in front of him darkly, frowning, 'We
are going on, pick up the traps!'

'Not me,' the boy growled. 'My shoulder hurts.'

The little girl threw back her head.

'Dirty fascist,' she said.

'They broke my shoulder!'

'They broke your nut!' the little girl cried in her fresh, ringing voice that spattered so coolly on the dusty, June ground, like a jet of cold water. 'If you don't come here at once I'll squash both your shoulders as if you were a bug!'

The three children trudged along the deserted street, one behind the other. Johnny walked in front. On one shoulder he carried a big overstuffed rucksack made of camouflage material that bumped against the backs of his knees, from the other a pair of huge leather slippers hung on a long string; he had covered his fair hair against sun and dust with a red scarf. Peter, walking behind him, balanced a green patched rucksack on his back, round his neck he carried the wire noose with which, after dark, he was wont to strangle any dogs and cats that came his way. His elbows stuck out from his torn shirt, his knees from his trousers. Behind the two of them walked the little girl, also with a full rucksack on her shoulder from the mouth of which a long wooden spoon stuck out. She swung a birch-rod in her hand and a full-blown poppy hung from her mouth. Neither spoke to the other, only Johnny, walking in front, muttered to himself the way old women and children wrangle, echoless, with their own loneliness.

Round the corner of the next crossroads a red brick Lutheran church loomed above the one-storey houses and a large, open area became visible beyond the mouth of the street.

'Turn in here, Johnny,' cried the little girl from behind. This street was also completely deserted, only a slowly descending cloud of dust showed that a dog must have run across the road a short while back. In the middle of the yellow lawn in front of the church a lonely sumac stood playing with its shadow. Further on, on the edge of the lawn, a broken rusty tank squatted on its wheelless axles; Johnny spat on it as he walked by. Peter stopped and examined it, but there was nothing left to strip off.

'Johnny, aren't you hungry?' the little girl cried from behind.

'Why shouldn't I be?' the child said.

'Do you want some cherries?'

The child frowned.

'If there are any maggoty ones,' he said after deliberating, 'I'll have them.'

The little girl ran forward. From the pocket of her skirt she palmed a handful of salmon-red cherries into the little boy's hand. The boy glanced at them suspiciously.

'I don't want them,' he said. 'They aren't maggoty.'

'You can still eat them,' the little girl murmured.

The boy made a face.

'I won't,' he said. 'I don't like them empty. Give them to Peter.'

A peasant in top-boots advanced towards them; he was there before them as suddenly as if he had risen out of the sun-warmed dust. He had a tiny, fair moustache, shaved closely on both sides, a vest and a blue flannel shirt and he carried a small basket, tied in a red kerchief, in his hand. The moment he reached Peter he stopped in his tracks and muttered an oath.

'Johnny, run!' the little girl screamed a second later.

The child looked back, then jumped into the air and broke into a run. Peter was too late; his long, black hair was caught in the peasant's hand. The little girl ran towards the other end of the street but as soon as she reached the opposite pavement she turned and tore back like the wind.

'Leave go of him!' she shouted, panting. Peter was sitting on the ground, the peasant had wound his long hair around his hand like a hemp-rope.

'I've caught you, you dirty scamp,' he growled, reaching with his right hand for the little girl who jumped up and down around him like a mother hen, defending her chickens, round a cat. The basket in its red kerchief sat in the dust a few feet away.

'Leave go of him!' the girl screeched, 'because if you don't I'll bring down the whole street on you, you filthy butcher! Let him go, do you hear? Or do you want us to pay for that horrible sour soup you gave us for supper last night? God will punish you, you sweaty-head, you won't die in your bed, don't count on it . . .'

The peasant pulled his hand out of Peter's rucksack and made a grab for her but by then the little girl was dancing behind his back.

'Let him go, you Hitler-moustache!' she screamed bringing the birch-rod down on the peasant's back. 'Aren't you ashamed to attack three fatherless-motherless orphans who earn their own living? Look how skinny we are, you pot-bellied swine! I bet you have bacon for breakfast, you grunting pig!'

The man couldn't run after her without letting go of Peter's hair who sat motionless, in a heap on the ground. He reached back with his hand but by then the little girl was swinging her skirt at the other side of him.

'Give back what you stole from me!' the peasant growled, his face bloated and blood-red.

'Filthy capitalist!' cried the little girl jumping back.

Big drops of sweat gleamed on both sides of the peasant's moustache. Sticking out her tiny behind the little girl bent forward mockingly.

'Melon-head!' she shouted in her crystal clear, sharp voice, 'Brood animal! Shit-on-the-ground! Big brute!'

The peasant looked at Peter sitting at his feet and with a jerk pulled him up by his hair.

'Let him go!' the little girl screamed at him, 'May your mother never speak to you again if you don't let him go!'

'What did you say?' the peasant growled and again he dug into Peter's rucksack. 'Give me back what you stole from me!'

The bells of the Lutheran church behind them were chiming midday; each chime churned up a little dust on the roofs of the houses and mixed it imperceptibly with the sunlight which then—like the pink cheeks of a bride under her veil—momentarily lost its colour and brilliance. A cart came clanking towards them from the end of the street with two skinny cows harnessed to its pole. The little girl threw a quick glance backwards, then she brought the birch rod down hard on the peasant's snatching hand.

'What do you want us to give you back?' she cried. 'The dollars? We've torn them up and thrown them away long ago. If we tell the police that we found dollars in your bed they'll keep you in prison until you go mouldy. You can bet your life the police wouldn't do anything to an orphan like me whose father and mother were taken away by the fascists! Only yesterday I sat on the sergeant's knee; he even gave me a cigarette!'

The boy sitting on the ground began unexpectedly to moan and whine. As if driven out of her mind by the sound the little girl leapt forward, her head bent, caught the man's hand and bit it with all her strength. A second later Peter was galloping away on the other side of the street while the peasant, swearing loudly, his face distorted with pain, ran in pursuit of the little girl. But in spite of the rucksack dancing on her back she raced along with such speed that the clumsy and heavily limping man soon lost sight of her.

Even as she ran the little girl kept her eyes peeled. She was not scared, her heart beat faster only from the strain put upon it by her speed, her fair hair fluttered gaily out behind

her. She watched both pavements carefully and had enough
presence of mind left to dispatch a cherry from her pocket to
her dried-out mouth. A few minutes later she caught sight of
Johnny in a distant doorway with the red kerchief, winking
from afar, on his head.

'This way, Tutyu!' the little boy shouted waving both
arms wildly.

The little girl glanced behind her but her pursuer had
submerged behind the dust.

'Here, hide in this doorway!' the child cried. 'Where's
Peter?'

'I saved him,' the little girl panted.

'How?'

'I bit the peasant.'

Johnny stared with round, shining eyes into the little girl's
freckled face.

'Where did you bite him?'

'In the throat,' the little girl said. 'I bit through his throat.'

'Did it bleed much?' Johnny asked. 'How much blood
came out of it? . . . Ten litres? . . . Why isn't your mouth
bloody?'

'I wiped it,' the little girl said. 'But inside it is still red.
Can you see it?'

She opened her mouth, the little boy tilted his head to
one side and inspected it carefully.

'It isn't very red,' he said in a disappointed voice after a
while. 'A dog bit me once and I bit it back but it stank and
my mouth was all full of hair.'

They met Peter an hour later at the Market place where
they were holding a National Fair on that very day.

'You dog-catcher,' the little girl said. 'I nearly got caught
because of you!'

'Because of me?'

The little girl nodded angrily.

'Didn't he have you by the hair?'

Peter flushed with fury.

'Wait till I have you by the hair,' he cried stamping his feet. 'I don't need your help, I can do all right without you! Don't you pick on me!'

'The devil picks on you,' the little girl said and turned away.

There were many people in the market but there was little to buy. The townswomen sat side by side in a long row with the sad leftovers of their households displayed at their feet, here and there among them a few peasant women caught the eye with a variety of junk, cherries, vegetables and cottage cheese in their baskets. Nobler products, eggs, bacon, poultry, were offered for sale only by those who wanted to settle their bank loans with the price of a pair of chickens or exchange twenty five eggs for a suit of clothes. In keeping with the slow supply, business was only just limping along and grew livelier only on the edge of the market, behind the backs of the stall-holders; here a few showpeople had set up their tents who would let you in even for money.

The three children stopped at one of the tents. It was a big one, made of camouflaged canvas, with a narrow wooden platform in front of it and a tiny box-office also built of boards. On the façade of the tent, in red letters on a black background, stood: BLOODY ADVENTURES OF THE PORTUGUESE PRINCESS.

'We're going in,' Peter said. Johnny held on tight to the little girl's hand.

The Portuguese king sat on the platform with long, grass-green hair streaming down to his shoulders from under his golden crown. His brows were also green in his aristocratically pale face and sombre corals, the colour of blood, hung from his ears on silver chains. His nose was somewhat fleshy and decorated with a few warts.

'That's the king,' the little girl explained.

'What kind of dress is he wearing?' Johnny enquired.

The little girl examined the costume closely.

'I don't know,' she said. 'A royal dress. The kind my sister wore when men came to see her at night.'

The child regarded the royal costume with awe. They were standing in the first row, a large crowd was pressing forward behind them, curious but closefisted. There was hardly any sound except the stamping of feet in the soft dust, a suppressed fidgeting and, from far away, the organ of the merry-go-round. But in the eyes of some of the younger spectators the Portuguese king grew immense and flashed like a diamond.

'What is he doing out here now?' Johnny asked. 'Ruling?'

The king's ear must have caught the question because he threw a furious glance at the child who, frightened, drew closer to the little girl.

'No,' she said, 'he can rule only inside, in the tent. There he is master over life and death, he can even have people beheaded if he wants to.'

'Us too?'

'Yes,' the little girl whispered, 'if we go in, us too. But out here the police won't let him.'

'Let's go in,' Johnny said, turning pale.

'Will you pay?' Peter asked the little girl.

At that moment the executioner appeared behind the king on the platform. He wore a blood-red coat with black buttons, red jersey pants ran down his spindly legs all the way to his red shoes, with curly tips like Venetian gondolas. He leaned with both hands on a blood-smudged, gold-hilted sword; the broad blade flashed in the sunshine as if it were interpreting for the people cruel and poetic messages from a distant heavenly body. Also the executioner's face was transcendentally pale and evil; in keeping with the rules of his craft he wore a big black beard which was moth-eaten in several places.

'Isn't he ugly!' a female voice exclaimed. Peter gave a frightened gasp and held on with both hands to the wooden platform. The people shifted their weight from one foot to the other in their amazement, someone dropped his cane.

'What does he have in his hand?' Johnny asked.

'A sword,' the little girl explained. 'He cuts people's heads off with a sword.'

'Why doesn't he make the king give him a sub-machine-gun?' Peter asked. 'You can work much faster with that.'

The little girl shrugged her shoulders.

'It's expensive,' she said. 'He probably doesn't have enough money. Besides, this looks better.'

'That's true,' Peter said biting his lips with excitement. 'Still, when I have money I'll buy a sub-machine-gun. With that you can liquidate a whole village in half an hour.'

The flap of the tent parted for a moment and out stepped a man in shirt-sleeves, with a top hat on his head and a red-ribboned drum resting on his belly. He had very long white fingers that worked the drumsticks with extraordinary speed. Immediately the throng turned to him and the cheerful quarrelsome rat-a-tat of the drum attracted people from the other, shadier side of the square as well. A Russian soldier stopped in front of the tent, tilted his cap back on his head and submitted the actors to careful scrutiny.

'Walk up, walk up,' the drummer cried, putting a temporary stop to his precise and playful dialogue with the drum. He spoke with a foreign accent which dressed his words in a guise as attractive and exciting as that worn by the king and the executioner; the king's scarlet cape which, in its off moments looked like a woman's dressing gown, blazed up suddenly as if ignited by the light of the foreign-sounding words.

'Walk up, ladies and gentlemen,' cried the drummer from under his top-hat, 'come and see the bloody adventures of the Portuguese princess, based on historical data, word for word just as they happened in the sixteenth century, with the original cast. The performance begins right away. This is the only stage that offers real art because we are acting this historical event on the basis of original documents and the young lady playing the Portuguese princess is even more beautiful than the original as everyone can establish from contemporary photographs. The king is played by Don Basilio, the most famous actor in the world, entirely free of charge, moved by his selfless enthusiasm for art. As for the executioner, he is not an actor, ladies and gentlemen, but a genuine executioner, whom we won away from the royal court of England after his five hundredth execution. As you can see, our performance surpasses reality in its historical authenticity, a hall-mark of real art. Walk up, ladies and gentlemen, we shall make an exception and accept cash which, in these days, is also a unique opportunity in its way. An egg per head will be accepted instead of cash for the Portuguese princess.'

The drummer resumed drumming with devilish speed, then the flaps parted again and another man in a top-hat stepped out onto the platform. He lifted a huge brass trumpet to his lips and blew so hard that the thunder-and-lightning tones made an old woman's nose bleed and the sparrows, bathing in the dust of the market-place flew off terrified in all directions. Several people made their way towards the box office.

'Are you going to treat us?' Peter asked in a shaky voice and shook his long black hair.

Johnny squeezed the hand of the little girl who turned pale with excitement.

'How much is a ticket?' she asked.

'Five million,' Peter, who could read, replied.

All three fell silent.

'It isn't much,' Johnny remarked after a while. 'Go on, fork out. We've done enough today.'

The throng stamped about enthusiastically in front of the box-office. A lad counted down banknotes on the sill of the narrow window with the anxious seriousness of a dog relieving himself. Behind him stood three peasant girls in starched skirts, shyly smiling; one of them wouldn't raise her eyes from the ground. Some paid in eggs or a little tobacco, and one old woman commuted art's levy for herself and her grandson into a pound of white bread.

'Where's the Princess?' a voice shouted in the background. 'Why don't you show her as well?'

The drummer pointed behind him with one of his drumsticks.

'The Princess won't show herself free of charge,' he cried in his impressive accent. The king, on the platform, broke into uproarious laughter. The crumbly sounds of gipsy music floated towards them from behind the whirling dust.

Holding on tight to each other the three children approached the box-office.

'Please let us go in for nothing,' the little girl said. A fat, yellow-haired woman sat behind the window.

'No,' the woman said.

'Please, let us in,' the little girl begged in a sing-song voice, 'we are orphans, everyone lets us in free.'

'No,' the woman said.

The little girl raised herself on tiptoe.

'If the king acts free of charge,' she said, 'you could let us in free of charge too.'

'No,' the woman said for the third time. A red-cheeked peasant woman in a black shawl holding a scrubbed-faced, freckled child in her arms stood behind the children.

'Let one in,' she suggested, 'so it can tell the others about it.'

The cashier shook her head in silence. The drummer released the running-belt of drumming. Peter took hold of the box-office window and shook it with all his might.

'I want to go in, lady!' he cried, his eyes overflowing with tears, 'please, let me go in!'

As the people behind them were getting restive, the little girl reached into her bosom and pulled out a large man's wallet from which she picked a sheaf of carefully folded banknotes. She put them down on the window sill.

'How much is that?' she asked. 'Is it enough yet?'

'What's that in your hand?' the cashier asked. 'Let me see!'

'Dollars,' the little girl said. 'A five dollar note.'

The lady held out her hand.

'Give it here!'

The little girl deliberated for a while, then held out the banknote. 'But you'll let all three of us in?' she asked.

Inside the tent it was dark, only through the slits in the canvas did blade-sharp beams of light stab in, revealing here the back of a chair, there a pale, moustachioed male face. The outlines of objects emerged slowly, reluctantly, from the solemn sawdust-smelling obscurity as if they had grown tired of exploiting human bodies and wanted to be left alone. After several jerky attempts, the curtain opened.

The Portuguese King sat on his golden throne in the left corner of the stage, dipping his thick feet in the scarlet cushions of the foot-stool. From the other corner of the stage a Knight, clad in black from top to toe and with a black plume on his helmet sped forward rattling his sword. In the background, through the wide open door, the park of the royal castle became visible, with an avenue of palms running straight towards the brilliant blue sea. At least a hundred palms stood one behind the other, growing smaller in the distance, but even the smallest was sharply separated from the others in the wonderful shell-blue light, and the avenue was so long that it would take at least half an hour to reach the shore, even on horseback.

'God almighty,' a deep, amazed voice said.

A female figure, walking along dreamily, appeared among the palms, one could see her slowly approaching the castle. At first she was no bigger than a thumb and yet one could clearly distinguish her nail-sized face with the tiny mouth, nose, eyes, and the brown hair streaming down to her shoulders. On her head she wore a thimble-sized green crown. Advancing slowly she grew larger and larger until, at last, she entered the door, life-size and smiling.

'It's the Princess,' the little girl whispered.

'But she isn't bloody !' said Johnny.

'Not yet,' she whispered back, 'she will be later.'

The audience was completely enthralled by the resplendence of the alien maritime landscape; there wasn't enough movement even to shake a cobweb. In the distance, diminutive sailing ships rocked on the tousled, sparkling sea, the sails whipped around like the corners of a handkerchief. Microscopic sailors sunned themselves on the miniature decks, under match-stick masts. By now the Princess was standing by the throne. She was so beautiful that the little girl felt her heart contracting.

'What language are they speaking?' Peter asked. 'German?'

The little girl shrugged, she didn't feel like answering. Johnny was watching with his whole body, bent forward in his seat, his fist pressed to his lips.

'What language are they talking?'

'Shut up !' Johnny whispered beside himself, 'Portuguese !'

'Why not Hungarian?'

'It wouldn't be so beautiful . . .' the little girl panted.

The conversation between the King and the Knight obviously concerned the Princess who stood trembling by the

throne in her wheat-coloured dress. The two great men were
eating from a large golden tray.

'Just look at that, they're eating sausage!' exclaimed a
surprised voice behind the children. And indeed, the King
was holding a long sausage between his fat fingers. At the
sight of the famliar food the whole audience drew a relieved
breath.

'It isn't true,' Johnny whispered, 'it isn't a sausage!'

'What then?'

'A banana.'

The little girl gave the child a grateful look.

'You're right,' she confirmed, 'banana. One eats only
bananas and birds from a golden plate.'

'What birds?'

'Eagles, and ostriches, and suchlike,' the little girl said.

The Black Knight asked the Princess to marry him but
she only stamped the ground with her gold slippers and
turned angrily away. So the good King, though he was sorry,
refused the suitor who hit his sword, threatened the king
with his fist, then departed swearing. The Princess blew her
little nose into a reseda-coloured handkerchief. The curtain
was drawn.

It grew dark again in the tent, people began to fidget in their
seats but nobody felt like talking. Here and there a young
couple would exchange a few whispers, boots creaked, the
older peasant lads stared woodenly at the curtain. The little
girl sat frowning, gazing quietly before her, like someone
watching a dream taking shape beyond space and filtering
it into life; her facial muscles tensed, her large, serious dark
eyes shone ecstatically and her toes curled in tensely. The
actors performed with such unequivocal, clear gestures that
there was no need for the explanatory ribbons of words;
every movement they made spoke straight to her excitedly
thumping heart. Her back was covered in goose pimples, her

little stomach and thighs in sweat. She became aware of the
two boys only when the curtain parted again and Johnny
moaned with happiness.

When the second act began the sun was still shining, the
King sat on his throne sleeping. He slept in Hungarian, his
snores were intelligible to all. The Princess was again walking among the palms.

'It smells good,' Johnny whispered, 'it must be the smell
of those trees.'

'It isn't,' Peter corrected him, 'it's the sea.'

'How do you know?'

'I've been on the sea,' the boy informed him. Johnny
groaned and tugged at the little girl's dress plaintively.

'He is lying again,' he whispered. 'Only Jews travel on the
sea, isn't that right?'

'Look!' the little girl said excitedly.

Beyond the Princess, deep within the avenue of palms, a
tiny black shadow fell on the road and then, from behind a
distant minute palm, the Black Knight emerged on tiptoe.
It was obvious that he was planning to abduct the Princess
but for the time being, because of the distance between them,
he seemed less than half as tall as the lady. His black armour
gleamed like the wing of a fly.

'Look out, he is coming!' Johnny exclaimed half aloud. 'He
is coming fast!'

The little girl clasped his hand in hers. 'She doesn't notice!'

Peter jumped up from his seat. 'I should hope not!'

'Why?'

'Let him abduct her!' hissed the long-haired boy viciously,
'Let him abduct her!'

In her excitement the little girl pressed her hand to her
stomach. Johnny rose.

'If she reaches the castle in time her daddy will protect
her.'

'She won't reach it,' Peter muttered, 'she won't reach it, she won't reach it! He is coming fast as hell!'

'And she still hasn't noticed him!' Johnny complained.

The little girl emitted a little scream then, pressing her palm on her lips, she too rose from her seat.

'He's got her!' Peter growled between his clenched teeth. 'By the hair! Hold her by the hair! Put your hand over her mouth!'

The audience sat in petrified silence.

'Mr. King, wake up!' Johnny shouted at the top of his voice. The little girl, pale as death, pulled him down on his chair and held his hand tight.

'You mustn't shout!' she whispered bending to the boy's ear. 'You'd protect me . . . you would, wouldn't you, if someone tried to abduct me?'

In the distance, in the shell-coloured light, a somewhat larger ship appeared among the white schooners, with blood-red sails and gleaming brass cannons on its deck. It glided towards the shore, swift as the wind, growing rapidly as it advanced until its pirate flag with skull and crossbones covered the whole blue sky. As soon as it reached the shore, an ant-sized human figure jumped from the deck.

'Who is that?' Johnny asked.

The little girl shook her head. As there were no sea pirates in the lowlands, no one for the moment could answer his question.

'Perhaps it's Horthy,' Johnny whispered uncertainly, 'he goes everywhere by boat!'

The Pirate had a long, fair moustache and long, fair hair just like the Princess. He drew his sword with a movement so proud that the blood froze in the audience's veins. The duel was fought at the foot of the first palm tree, immediately in front of the castle gate; the little red lips of the trembling Princess were sealed with a black kerchief and inside, in the throne room, the good King snored stertorously, untroubled. The blades clashed like eagles' wings.

'Kill him, blackie!' Peter cried.

Now one retreated, now the other, the children stamped their feet, their faces livid, their nostrils quivering.

'Jesus Christ, save me,' the little girl prayed silently. If the Black Knight wins she is lost, she thought.

On her left Johnny wheezed like a threshing machine, on her right Peter beat the back of the fat peasant woman sitting before him with his fist.

'Go on, blackie, kill him!' he shouted uninterruptedly; he was frothing at the mouth.

The little girl began to cry:

'What a wicked boy you are,' she told him and closed her eyes.

After a while she had to shut them again: when the executioner dragged the Black Knight to the scaffold and then, in full sight of the audience, cut his head off with his broad sword. Before his execution the Black Knight raised his index finger, rattled his chains and laughed like a devil.

'Wham,' said Johnny, 'he's cut it off. Like a chicken. Why are you shutting your eyes?'

The little girl opened one eye and stole a glance at the castle, the good King was watching the execution from his throne and drinking wine from a bejewelled chalice. The huge red globe of the setting sun hovered close above the surface of the sea and steeped the slender avenue and the friendly throne room in the colour of blood.

'Look, the executioner is swinging the head!' Johnny said. 'Bam, now he's thrown it into a basket.'

'Is he no longer alive?' the little girl asked, her eyes still shut.

'No,' Johnny said, 'he fell behind the table. Only his feet are sticking out.'

The little girl took a deep breath and let go the arm of the chair. Peter was sitting at her side humped, his elbows on his knees, gazing before him with dull eyes. The little girl turned her eyes away stiffly. She looked closely at Johnny: the boy's pale face was flushed, his eyes shone with tears, his upper lip had grown wet with all the excitement. The little girl wiped it with her skirt and kissed him, and her heart swelled with great courage.

Up there, in the throne room, the last big scene was unfolding. The good King forgave the Pirate his innumerable crimes. He took him by the hand, led him to the Princess, and put their hands into each other's. The Princess smiled shyly. The palms swayed gently in the evening breeze dropping small dates onto the pebbles of the walk. The Pirate . . .

The little girl cried out in pain.

'What is he doing?' she whispered pressing both small fists on her heart. 'What's the matter with him?'

The two boys were also watching these events uncomprehendingly. The Pirate stepped back, bowed deeply before the Princess, then, straightened up and shook his head vigorously.

'Why is he shaking his head?' Johnny asked.

'He is shaking his forefinger as well!'

Peter stiffened. 'Doesn't he want the skirt?'

'Is he ill?' the little girl asked, panting.

Again all three jumped up from their seats.

'He must be ill,' Johnny said, 'because he is beating his heart.'

'But why is he pointing to the sea?' the little girl whispered.

'He is pointing to his ship.'

'That isn't true,' Peter said, 'it isn't his ship, he is pointing to the whole sea, look how he waves his arm.'

'And now he is pointing at the sun!' Johnny cried.

The little girl's mouth filled with saliva, her knees tingled.

'He doesn't want the Princess,' she stammered in a dying voice and big tears sprang to her eyes.

'Well, what does he want?'

'The sea,' said Johnny. 'He doesn't want to sit at home all the time in a big stone castle.'

'Is that why he keeps slapping his chest?'

'Hell . . .' Peter growled discontentedly, 'what is he doing now? He has spread his arms wide and is looking up to the sky.'

'He'll fly away!' Johnny cried excitedly.

'Where to?'

'Far away! . . . To the negroes.'

The little girl sank back, exhausted. She did not believe that the beautiful, wavy-haired, fair Pirate would take to wings and fly away but she did see that he wanted to be his own master.

'You can see now,' Peter whispered gloatingly, bunching his fists with anger, 'it was a pity to execute the Black Knight. What did they gain by it? Damn all! . . .'

Once more the Pirate pressed his hand to his heart then, waving his hat, he marched away towards the distant home of freedom! The Princess's tiny reseda-coloured handkerchief fluttered after him like a chained butterfly. A moment later the departing figure disappeared in the golden dust of the sun. The curtain closed.

'There you are,' a thick voice said, 'he showed her!'

Shuffling, people were slowly getting ready to leave. Their palms were wet, their feet leaden, the cold ashes of snuffed-out excitement settled on their hearts. Robust terrestrial light and dust streamed in through the open flap of the tent. The women blinked, the men cleared their throats. The three children remained last under the overheated canvas, fumbling with their rucksacks and staring at the impenetrable green velvet curtain. Coming out of the tent they stopped for a moment; in the strong sunshine the wide market-place appeared immense and stupid, the air was lustreless, the acacia trees disorderly, Hungarian words flat. They tramped on side by side silently, their eyes on the ground.

'Where are we going?' Peter asked.

'We are getting out of this town.'

'Fine,' Johnny said. 'Do you know the way?'

'We go where the wind blows,' the little girl said.

The street ran straight toward the railway station, then, skirting it where the warehouses stood, opened, at the turnpike, onto the high street. It was a concrete road, its accumulated heat burned one's bare soles.

'Put on your sandals,' the little girl told Johnny.

'Tutyu,' he asked, 'have you ever been to the theatre?'

The little girl shook her head. 'That was the first time.'

'I've been,' Peter informed them.

'Where?'

'In Budapest,' the boy said. 'I went to the theatre every day there.'

Johnny looked at the little girl, she winked back at him. They understood each other. Neither replied to the long-haired boy; his fate was sealed.

'The Knight wasn't dead,' Peter said. 'When the blonde sailor was talking to the Princess, he moved his feet twice.'

A small, dusty whirl-wind rose before them, chasing its own tail like a dog. In the steep rays of the sun the black shadows of the poplars stood like puddles around the feet of the trees; the little girl dipped her foot into them.

'Don't you believe me?' Peter asked.

'No,' Johnny answered firmly.

Peter broke into an ugly laugh.

'Dope!' he said. 'If he had died who would act at the next performance? Eh, Tutyu?'

Half an hour later they reached a cross-roads one corner of

which was decorated with a toppled crucifix and a rusting
German tank. The little girl stopped by the tank.

'Aren't you talking to me?' Peter asked.

'No,' the little girl said.

'Why not?' asked the long-haired boy.

The little girl's eyes suddenly narrowed, her forehead
turned old.

'This is where we part,' she said curtly.

'Who?'

'We ... from you!'

'How come?'

'We don't need you,' the little girl said.

The boy stared rigidly before him, his long black hair fell
over one eye.

'You don't need me?' he repeated unbelievingly. 'Why
don't you need me?'

The little girl swung her birch rod.

'You are just as evil as the Knight,' she said in a toneless
voice. 'You have strangled three dogs since we've been together. I don't want anyone like you.'

Peter turned livid with fury.

'And you thought of this today?' he screeched, 'on this
blessed day? Why today of all days?'

'I don't know,' the little girl said. 'I've just decided.'

They stared at each other silently. The boy's lower lip
shook, he turned blue with anger, the wire loop around his
neck threatened to snap.

'We blew all our money this afternoon and there's nothing else to share, right? Get going, worm!'

'Go to hell,' Peter said making a face. 'You're not serious,
are you?'

'I am,' the little girl said.

Peter began to swear. He swore so filthily that Johnny
blushed with shame. The little girl listened in silence.

'I won't beat you up,' she said, 'because you don't belong
to us any longer. But get going now !'

Johnny and she waited at the shot-up tank until Peter's
rapidly diminishing figure with the swollen rucksack on its
back disappeared behind the dust. Johnny was chewing a
piece of dry bread indifferently, the little girl brought out
a comb and a brush from her rucksack and combed the
boy's hair. They then took each other by the hand and set
out.

'Was the Princess more beautiful than me?' the little girl
asked.

'Much more beautiful,' Johnny said firmly.

The little girl meditated for a while.

'She had beautiful big breasts,' Johnny explained, 'and you
haven't got any. In her ears she had diamonds as big as eggs,
there wasn't a single freckle on her nose, and her dress was
all silk and velvet.'

'Then it's all right,' the little girl said, relieved, 'then it
wasn't me, after all.'

Johnny laughed loudly, heartily.

'Of course it wasn't you !' he laughed. 'Your legs are dirty
and hers were as white and lovely as cotton wool.'

'Did you see those tiny sailors on the ship?' the little girl
asked. 'All of them would have served her.'

'There were Chinese among them and Russians and French,'
Johnny hummed. 'And negroes. And they had a soccer team,
too.'

'On the ship?'

'Yes,' Johnny said. 'Between the masts there was a little
football pitch and that's where they played with a tiny
golden ball.'

The little girl looked out over the fields burned yellow by
the sun; there was not a single soul in sight for miles. For
a while she dug around in her pocket absent-mindedly, then

she took a cigarette from a tin box and a brass lighter and lit the cigarette.

'There was a golden bird on top of one of the masts. It sang,' she said blowing ribbons of smoke from her snub nose.

Johnny nodded.

'I heard it,' he said. 'The centre-half was Hungarian.'

They advanced slowly, comfortably, the wind kicked up tiny clouds of dust before them.

'A big, red, crested fish swam round the ship,' Johnny said, 'and when the ball fell into the water he threw it back.'

'It was a Persian chin-chin fish,' the little girl said drawing on her cigarette.

Her thin, little freckled face was serious and passionate like a child's at a feast. The rucksack had bruised her shoulder but apart from that she didn't feel her body; though she didn't know it herself, she was busy reforming the world. Between two rows of whispering poplars the road ran straight as an arrow towards a fleecy cloud.

'Where are we going to sleep tonight?' Johnny asked.

'On the ship,' the little girl said.

'Fine,' the boy murmured. 'We'll sign up as sailors. Can I have a piece of bread?'

A GAY FUNERAL

A GAY FUNERAL

WHENEVER Mrs. V. got excited, she immediately started to stutter. When greatly upset, she stammered. Ever since her husband's condition had turned critical it was only with great difficulty and after several attempts that she could utter words beginning with a consonant; and at such times she would, in her nervousness, push anyone she was talking to in the chest, when walking in the street she'd sweep people out of her way, or, sitting at a table she'd brush off with her arm any coffee cup, flower vase, or ashtray placed before her. She considered the impending demise of her husband so extraordinary an event that in its forward and backward cast shadow, she felt entitled to offend against all the rules of behaviour; it was up to the world to respect her state of mind.

When the doctor came out of the sick-room she made him sit down beside her on the davenport though he was obviously in a hurry.

'A cup of coffee?'

'Thank you, no,' the doctor replied. 'I'm in a hurry.'

The woman turned her tearstained face toward him.

'It's just being made. It'll be ready in a minute.'

'If you wish,' the doctor said.

'What news?'

The doctor shrugged.

'No improvement at all?'

'Improvement?'

Tears overflowed from the woman's beautiful, velvety-brown eyes, ran down both sides of her charmingly pert, if now somewhat puffy nose, and dripped down on her skirt.

'Dear doctor,' she said, 'dear doctor! I shall never give up hope. Do give me a word of comfort!'

The old, bald-headed doctor drew his hand slowly from between the woman's two soft clutching palms.

'Perhaps he has another week.'

'A week? Ridiculous!' the woman said. 'You mean to say a year, don't you?'

As soon as the doctor had gone, she telephoned her dressmaker, ordered a black costume and insisted that it be ready in two days.

She spoke loudly, excitedly.

'I cannot w . . . w . . . w . . . wait any longer,' she stammered. 'The ca . . . ca . . . catastrophe might occur tomorrow, don't you understand? I don't mind what you do but it must be ready or you'll never see me again as long as you live!'

She shouted so excitedly that the three black-clad old women sitting in the room, all three of them distant relatives, who had been crouching round the table during the doctor's visit, motionless, breathless, soundless—looming shadows of three future mourners—simultaneously looked up, raised their brows and lifted their arms.

'Not so loud,' they whispered, 'he might hear you!'

Bozsi, the fifty-year-old servant, brought in the clothes that had to be taken down to the cleaners immediately for a 24-hour dyeing service. There was a brick-coloured woollen coat lined with steel-blue stuff. The lining would have to be removed, it was expensive material. A pink and a white silk blouse, a burberry suit. A pink Italian raw silk frock.

'Peep in, Matild, and see if the injection has made him sleep yet,' said the widow-to-be to one of the old women. 'He likes a sleep about now. I don't want him to catch sight of my tearstained face.'

By the time Matild returned from the sick-room the woman
had hung the pink raw silk frock with trembling hands back
in the wardrobe.

'But Madam will never be able to wear this again!' said the
servant.

The woman turned her back on the maïd.

'Do you know, Matild, what this frock cost me?'

'No.'

'I don't remember,' the woman said. 'A fortune. Just touch
this silk. And what if he doesn't die?'

Matild looked at the silk, took it between two fingers,
pinched it. It was a heavy, soft material, full of electricity, it
almost sparkled under one's hand, one could have stroked it
for hours. The sunshine streaming in through the window lit
up in it the pink colours of the dawn that illuminated the
faces of the three old women bent over it.

'Lovely silk,' said Aunt Roza, the second old woman. 'Send
it down to the cleaners, child, you can't wear that again.'

The woman hung the frock back in the wardrobe. 'I have
faith,' she cried in her strong, agreeable voice. 'I have faith,
Aunt Roza!'

V. had been ailing for a year and a half. Two months
before, when he took to his bed for good, Professor X., the
country's greatest authority, a cancer specialist of European
fame, had told the woman that her husband was incurable.
His body was so weakened that he wouldn't last longer
than a week or two, but death might occur any day, from
one minute to the next. The woman listened to him unbeliev-
ing, tearless, she shook her head mutely and, in her heart,
disowned the professor. Two months had gone by since and
though it was a medical impossibility, V. was still alive.

'You are right, my dear,' said Aunt Berta, the third old
woman, a fat widow whose head shook nervously and whose
thin whining voice stuck to one's face and hair when she

spoke, twined itself round one's neck like duckweed, 'you are right. Don't you listen to the doctors. Had you listened to them our Ödön would have been in his grave long ago.'

For the last ten years Aunt Berta had made a living out of agreeing with Mrs. V. Lacking a well thought-out strategical plan and possessed of equal hate for the cunning Aunt Berta, the other two old women squatted side by side on a quiet little opposition bench and when it became unequivocally, clearly evident that the shaky-headed widow had encouraged the woman to do something which she later regretted, they both jumped on her.

'Haven't I always said so!' Aunt Matild, who hadn't said anything, would cry.

'And I, didn't I say so too?' Aunt Roza, who hadn't said anything either, would murmur, casting a look of such triumph on Aunt Berta that the latter's white head would immediately begin to shake. After a while she would rise, offended, and retire into the sick-room there to nurse her pain. Apart from this, all three of them got along well in their humble hatred of Mrs. V.

The woman ordered a taxi and left the dying man in the care of the three old women who would be joined by numerous visitors later, to drive into town to her milliner's to order a black hat with veil. Just as she was about to leave the telephone started ringing.

Aunt Matild, who was on telephone duty, lifted the receiver. When it was someone of minor importance she would impart information as to the patient's condition, she would— if the situation demanded it—avert the visit of insignificant acquaintances and modest friends, and find some excuse for the woman's absence if it so happened that at noon the latter was still in her bath or taking her after-lunch nap. However, she was forbidden to converse with persons of importance.

'Thank you, he is not too bad,' said the woman, who had

returned from the door, into the receiver. Her voice was dull, shot through with suffering.

'I am sur . . . sur . . . surprised, my dear Gyöngyi that you forgot to send us tickets for tomorrow's f . . . f . . . first-night. If Ödön knew he would be really upset, I didn't even tell him . . . Why shouldn't we come? Will you tell me? It is quite possible, of course, that Ödön won't be in the mood, or will be too busy, for he is working hard on his memoirs nowadays, still, you might have thought of me. Yes, me. You thought Ödön's condition was serious . . . !' Her voice became suddenly deep, with a tragic vibration. 'Yes, this is to be my fate one day, when I'm left alone, I know . . . All right, all right! Give my love to Janos.'

At the milliner's, she tried on several black-veiled models, chose one, then telephoned her home to ask whether the patient was sleeping peacefully. Black nylons proved more difficult to acquire. She found no black stockings at Mrs. S.'s who sold genuine English tweeds, French perfumes and American nylon undies at her Szemere Street flat. She telephoned round all the better-known stockists of smuggled goods in town, but in vain. With deadly exhaustion in her heart, because the struggle with death, topped by another ten worries a day, far surpassed her physical and mental strength, the woman called a taxi and drove home. She had ordered the typist for three o'clock, so the patient had to be awakened from his sleep at half past two sharp to be put into shape for work with a caffeine injection she herself administered.

Four or five visitors were sitting in the living room. A quick glance told her they were all unimportant.

'Is he asleep?'

'Yes.'

'Any telephone calls?'

'They are all written down. Nothing of importance, child.'

'Has the needle been sterilized?'

But the servant was already following her in, carrying the black ebony tray and on it, in a stainless steel receptacle, the hypodermic needle, a small bottle of alcohol, and a glass container filled with sterilised cotton wool. Still in her coat and hat, the woman hurried into the sick-room; the typist would be here in twenty minutes, by then the patient had to have the strength and the desire to work.

'Is lunch ready?' she asked as she came out of the sick-room.

*   *   *

New visitors had come to swell the ranks of those already in the living-room. In addition to the three old women, another four of five women sat whispering round the table laid for one, their chairs pulled slightly back to indicate that they had no wish to participate in the meal. Next to the china-cabinet, in the corner, an elderly, grey-haired man sat in a brocade-covered armchair, reading a book held close to his eyes. Two people were sitting on the red davenport, a former countess in a threadbare dress patched at the elbows, and a bent man, thin as a herring, once the editor of a banned Catholic periodical. All those present, including the daughter of a famous criminologist, now deported, and the wife of a well-known gynaecologist, now in prison, were getting money from the V.s.

Mrs. V. was kind-hearted. Her heart leaned mainly towards former notabilities, more or less famous names of a defunct social order, but at times she would not shy back from more modest misfortunes either. Promising young artists could always count on her soft hand. Fundamentally, she disliked giving something for nothing and, therefore, she usually demanded some counter-service, though she would then pay for it many times over. She collected small works of art and antiques—the dining room and living room walls were decorated up to the ceiling with terracotta figurines, plaquettes, crystal goblets; here an old chasuble hung on the wall, there a Turkish scimitar, and her generosity could always be triggered off by a modest offer for purchase of an old button that could be worked into a ring, or a family Bible belonging to the Andrassys. Everyone was familiar with the story of the young painter who sold her a small stone statue, for one thousand *forints*, which, as could be proven, had been seen by the poet Petöfi. The statue came from the gateway-arch of the building opposite the Café Pilvax.

'Why tomato soup?' she asked the servant. 'You know that I loathe it.'

'But Madam ordered it herself this morning!'

'Why do you ask me?' the woman said irritably. 'You know perfectly well that nowadays I am not accountable for what I am doing. Don't ask me, I have other things to worry about. Matild, where is the list of telephone calls?'

Aunt Matild smoothed the crumpled sheet of paper out on the table and the woman studied it attentively while spooning her soup. There wasn't a single name that merited being called back. While she read, she disposed of two plates of soup by the time Bozsi entered with the second course, stewed beef with onions, mashed potatoes, and pickled cucumber.

While the lady of the house had her lunch, the visitors chatted undisturbed. Some left, others came to take their place. There was constant coming and going in the room. The widow of a lord-lieutenant who received a monthly donation of 100 *forints* from the V.s, fell asleep in the corner of the davenport; at times she moaned in her sleep. The grey-haired man reading in the armchair rose, put the book back on the shelf, chose another, sat down again and went on reading. Others remained for a short while only, some arrived with the second plate of tomato soup and took their leave at the pudding; they didn't mind the long journey and the bus-fare to the Pasaret in order to figure on the imaginary visitors' list. It was well known that Mrs. V. kept a close check on every visit and every absence.

'Where is our poor Ödön to be buried?' asked a fat woman, the widow of the chairman of the former British-Hungarian Bank who was known for her crude outspokenness and who had returned from deportation just two weeks before. She wore high boots, a stiff collared shirt-waist and very short hair, well smoothed down: everyone knew that she was an ardent follower of Sappho. The V.s gave her a hundred or a hundred and fifty *forints* a month.

'Where?' the woman asked raising her head, 'where? In the Kerepes Cemetery, of course.'

'Hush, hush . . . it is early to talk of that yet, milady,' nodded Aunt Berta, suddenly changing the vertical trembling of her head into a horizontal pendulum movement. 'What on earth are you thinking about? Who is talking about funerals?'

The widow did not deign to answer her.

'At Kerepes? It will be difficult.'

'Difficult? . . . Why?'

'It's reserved for the dead of the State, old girl,' the woman said. 'How are you, Aunt Matild? I hear you've won five thousand *forints* on your peace-loan ticket.'

'I?' cried Aunt Matild, her face turning livid. 'I? Who told milady such a lie?'

'It isn't true then? I'm sorry. I was thinking of touching you for a hundred. When the Americans come, I'll repay you in dollars.'

The typist, a pale bespectacled girl, arrived. Mrs. V. looked at the clock: she was twenty minutes late.

'I'll be compelled to give him another caffeine shot because of you. You know very well that the effect lasts only for two hours. How long can you work now? Hardly an hour and a quarter . . .'

'That'll be enough for him, five minutes before the funeral,' said the fat widow.

At the word 'funeral' the lord-lieutenant's widow started up from her agreeable nap as if an alarm had gone off, smiled and looked around with a pleasurable yawn. Of all those present it was she who rested on the relatively most secure financial basis; her daughter had married an American air force officer and now sent her a regular stream of 'IKKA' parcels, coffee, cocoa, rum, Gillette blades, nylons, and, in separate packages, second-hand clothes which she sold, through an intermediary, to the wife of a cabinet minister. The coffee, cocoa and rum were taken off her hands by Mrs. V. at prices somewhat higher than the market ones. At times, Mrs. V. would even owe the old lady money so that, apart from the servant who sometimes didn't get paid for months, she was the only 'creditor' in that army of invaders who kept the V.'s home under permanent siege.

'A propos,' said the woman, starting up suddenly from her peaceful after-lunch doze, 'don't you have a pair of black nylons for sale? One can't get black nylons in this whole town. Terrible conditions! Don't you have a pair?'

'I'm sorry . . .'

The woman looked at the widow's legs.

'Aren't those nylons?'

'Which?'

'The ones you are wearing.'

'My only pair, darling.'

'I'll give you two hundred *forints* for them,' the woman said. 'Go on, make up your mind! I can't go to the funeral in smoke-coloured stockings. Take them off right away, I'll give you another pair instead, into the bargain!'

Modestly turning her back on the assembled company, the

widow pulled the nylons off her thick, varicose-vein covered
legs and put on the exchange pair. Meanwhile the servant
cleared the table. 'Black coffee?' she asked the woman in a
low voice. The woman looked around: There was no one
there deserving to be thus honoured.

'Only for me . . . and let milady have 200 *forints*! . . .
What do you mean, you have no money left? Only yesterday . . .'

The criminologist's daughter took her leave, a new visitor
entered the door.

'Another cup of coffee, Bozsi!' the woman shouted after
the servant. The new visitor, a tabetic young man with a thin
neck and a huge cranium, was one of the best known painters
in the capital and one of the more infrequent guests; he came,
mostly, to check whether his paintings hadn't been moved
from the place he had chosen for them, and whether no
place had become vacant to take another of his paintings, or
at least a drawing. He rated a cup of coffee.

'Have you heard what Radio Free Europe had to say yesterday?' he asked in his high, mocking voice, arranging his
jerky legs under the table.

All of them listened to Radio Free Europe. And yet, they
turned their careworn faces towards him.

'Don't you know?' The painter laughed. 'It is unbelievable
how many stupid, or let us say, naïve, people there still are
in the world and especially,' he glanced around, 'in our circles.
My janitor wouldn't swallow half of what we imbibe every
single day. That there has been an uprising of the Csepel
workers! A strike at Szolnok! . . . Yes, thank you, another
cup. It's very fortunate that a Paris janitor, on the other hand,
would not swallow half of what we'd ram down his throat.
Beautiful balance isn't it?'

'Beautiful?' a voice asked.

'The world survives on unbelief, isn't it so, my devout

friend?' said the painter turning to the neo-Catholic editor. 'That's the real constructive force ... How is Ödön?'

'Thank you, very much better,' said the woman.

'He doesn't believe in death, either,' the painter nodded with satisfaction and looked around.

The servant carried a silver tray bearing a small glass of cream, a little caviar on a plate, a glass of champagne, and in a third glass, some crushed ice, into the sick-room. The tapping of the typewriter, audible even through the padded door, ceased. But a moment later a rattling breath, subdued sounds, the eructation, rasping, of a convulsed larynx, were heard from the sick-room: the patient was vomiting. The door opened and the servant ran through the living-room, her face red, her eyes full of tears, to return a second later with a basin and a towel in her hands. The woman jumped up from the table and disappeared behind the padded door.

'He cannot swallow a mouthful without bringing it up immediately, poor soul,' said Aunt Roza.

'He hasn't taken a thing for three days,' Aunt Matild said.

'That isn't true,' said Aunt Berta, 'night before last he drank half a glass of lemonade.'

Bozsi, the servant girl, came out of the sick-room. At the door she stopped for a moment with the basin and towel in her hand, as if about to say something. She threw a disturbed glance at the company, her face burning with excitement. But she obviously changed her mind and left the room without uttering a word.

Several of the visitors seized the opportunity to depart.

*   *   *

The telephone rang.

'Unfortunately,' said the wife of the playwright, 'unfortunately the theatre has sent out all the tickets, I could

only get one, and even that with great difficulty. Do you
want it? Anyway, you said that Ödön wanted to work.'

'Of course,' said the woman.

'Shall I have it sent?'

'Yes, please,' said the woman. 'Who is sitting next to me?'

'I cannot tell you,' replied the voice in the telephone irritably. 'How should I know?'

The woman wiped her tearfilled eyes with the back of her
hand.

'Forgive me, Gyöngyi, darling,' she said, 'I'm terribly sensitive these days, I cannot sit next to just anyone. Perhaps
you could find out at the theatre who has the seat beside
mine. If you find out, get them to ring me. You and your
husband must really come and see us! Ödön is always talking about you.'

Only a few visitors had remained at their post, the standing
guests of the house. New visitors would appear only after
dinner. The woman took off her shoes, lay down on the
davenport, covered her legs with a light chequered red-and-
yellow plaid. She liked to take her after-lunch nap beneath
the quiet hum of a conversation going on above her head,
but this time, for some reason, she seemed excited and couldn't
fall asleep. After a while she raised herself on one elbow
and, with a gesture, summoned the wife of the gynaecologist
who was serving a four year sentence, a tall, scraggy, vulture-
nosed woman, to her side.

'Did you know this too?'

'Know what?'

'What?' the woman said irritably. 'That they're not taking
any more into the Ke . . . Ke . . . Kerepes Cemetery!'

'So I've heard.'

'Rubbish!' said the woman. 'Of course, they can't take
everybody in . . . Ilona!'

Ilona, a retired 'tragédienne' of the National Theatre, rose

from her armchair and tramped heavily over to the davenport. 'What is it, darling?'

'Have you heard that the Kerepes Cemetery is full up?'

'Yes, darling,' the actress said. 'The last one to be buried
there was the actor Somlay. Now only Communists get in.
The dead of the nation. Andor Gabor . . . Lajos Nagy . . .
Tibor Déry . . .'

'Tibor Déry! . . . But he isn't dead yet!' the woman cried.

'Of course he is dead!' the actress intoned, modulating her
voice in the best tradition of tragic playacting. 'I was at his
funeral. There was a great to-do, Revai spoke at the
grave . . .'

'Ma . . . ma . . . Matild!' the woman cried.

The three old women sat round the table with velvet-
smooth soles and withdrawn claws ready to jump. Aunt
Matild reached the head of the davenport in one leap.

'Did you know, too, that the Kerepes Cemetery is full up?'

'What is it you want, dear?' asked the old woman bending
over the davenport.

'Is it true that the Kerepes Cemetery is full up?'

'Of course,' said Aunt Matild, 'I know it is. But then Ödön
told us long ago that he wanted to rest in the Farkasret
Cemetery.'

The woman sat up.

'Rubbish,' she said. 'Ödön must get the place that is due
to him, and I'll see that he does. Roza! Have you heard as
well that the Kerepes Cemetery . . .'

'Don't upset yourself, dear heart,' said Aunt Roza at the
foot of the davenport. 'What is there to get excited about in
the fact that the politicians reserve a cemetery for themselves?
The Farkasret is nearer to us anyway, from Moscow Square
you can get there . . .'

The woman donned her shoes, rose and went to the telephone. Aunt Berta, the third old woman, who had remained

at the table, unasked and therefore deeply offended, sprang
up from her place and ran to the telephone.

'Shall I call the number, dearie?'

The woman looked at her. 'I suppose you've heard too
that . . .'

'It is full up, it is full up,' the old woman mumbled. 'And
so what, if it is full up? There isn't a glass of water so full
that it can't take another drop. And if, God forbid, it should
be full, can't somebody be disinterred?'

'Madam,' said the servant who had in the meantime come
into the room, 'will you come out for a second?'

'What for?'

'The old lady wants a word with Madam.'

An obese, grey-haired woman was sitting on the glass
porch opening onto the back garden with a cherry-red knitted
cap on her short, yellowish hair. She was the widow of one
of the Under-Secretaries for Home Affairs in the one-time
Bethlen cabinet and for the last few months—ever since V.'s
condition had worsened and work had become heavy around
the house, she had been coming in to help Bozsi with the
cleaning and washing-up as a daily. She received breakfast,
lunch, and five *forints* an hour. Unfortunately she was unable
to keep on with the work, she told Mrs. V., they had better
look for another daily.

'But . . . but . . . but, why?' the woman asked, petrified.

'I just can't go on, my dear,' the old lady declared resting
her chin on the silver-headed cane she held between her thick,
widespread knees.

Mrs. V. threw her a desperate glance from under her reddened, swollen lids. This on top of all her troubles, she
thought. It never rains but it pours.

'But why . . . why, milady?' she asked in a shaky voice.
'Have we offended you in any way?'

'I don't owe you any explanation, my dear,' said the old

lady in a cool, dignified, voice. She stretched out her thick
legs, and tapped with her cane on the toe of one of her shoes.

'Sorry!' said the woman, offended.

Inside, the telephone was ringing. Mrs. V. turned involuntarily and took half a step toward the door. The old lady
tapped the floor with her cane.

'If you don't mind, we can settle up, my dear,' she said.

The woman turned back.

'What do you mean?'

'I am asking for what is due to me,' the old woman said.
'I hope there were no complaints about my work?'

'You won't come tomorrow?' the woman cried. 'You desert
me from one moment to the next, milady? When my husband
is dying in the next room?'

The old lady continued to tap her shoes.

'Am I supposed to run after another dai . . . another help
now?' the woman continued in despair. 'From one day to the
next? When milady knows very well that nowadays the
dai . . . the helps steal one's eyes out of one's head?'

'Don't shout, my dear,' the old lady said. 'I don't like it
when ladies forget their manners. If I am rightly informed,
there is no need to give notice if you are employed by the
hour, so I'm quite within my rights to stop work at any
moment.'

'That is so,' the woman said biting her lip. 'So you are
giving notice, milady?'

The widow broke into a mocking smile. 'I am giving
notice.'

'And you're stopping work today?'

'I'm stopping today,' the old lady said, 'if you have no
objection.'

Inside the telephone rang again.

'I should like to state again,' the widow said, 'that there
were no complaints about my work.'

The woman turned to face the old lady and drew her lips in a pout.

'No special complaints,' she said easily, in a calm voice. 'The dishes were a bit dirty.'

'What?' mumbled the old lady and rose slowly, painfully, leaning on her cane. 'What?'

Mrs. V. put her hand on the knob of the kitchen door. 'It doesn't matter. They were a little dirty,' she repeated. 'You'll have to come back on Saturday for your money. As you know, I always pay on Saturday. Good day.'

'Don't you know what the matter is with her?' she asked the servant in the kitchen. From the lobby they heard the widow slamming the door. 'Don't you know?'

The servant blushed and lowered her eyes.

'Out with it! What are you afraid of?'

'What good is it to Madam to know,' Bozsi said blushing anew. 'Madam has enough to worry about without it.'

Mrs. V. hit the table with her palm.

'Stop fooling!'

'Too many Jews are coming to this house,' Bozsi said in a very low voice, keeping her eyes on the point of her shoes. 'She says she cannot get used to such company. She was going to leave last week but then I persuaded her to stay on at least until the Master dies. I don't know what got into her today.'

Inside the telephone started ringing again.

'Wha . . . what's the matter with this telephone?' cried the woman beside herself, tearing open the door. 'What time is it? Don't they know th . . . th . . . that I sleep at this hour?'

Aunt Matild was holding out the receiver to her. 'It's the notary. He says you called him.'

'Yes, it is I. Good afternoon,' said the woman into the receiver. 'I called you, Comrade, because unfortunately it cannot be put off any longer. I can tell you that his condition is such, that the catastrophe might occur from one hour to the next. Yes, his will should be made today. I'll give him a caffeine shot and vitamins and if you arrive within half an hour or an hour he will be in a condition to talk.'

Throughout this conversation, she felt the surprised glances of the three old women fixed on her back.

'But he has already deposited his will with his lawyer!' they cried almost simultaneously when she turned back. Aunt Matild raised her arms to the sky, Aunt Roza joined her hands as if she were praying, and Aunt Berta's head shook more than usual.

The woman sighed deeply, her knees turned to jelly in her excitement and she dropped into the nearest armchair.

'Dear Aunt Matild, Aunt Roza, Aunt Berta,' she said in a low voice, 'this has to be done. I don't know what that will contains. I cannot know whether he hasn't made another one. But if he makes a new will now, that invalidates all former wills.'

The notary arrived at a few minutes to six, by chance simultaneously with a young painter, Flora Jendrasik, a distant relative of Erno Jendrasik, the neurologist. The notary proceeded directly into the living room but Flora, who noticed that the servant's eyes were swollen with weeping, sat down in the kitchen.

'What's the trouble, Bozsi?' she asked.

The maid stood before her, her arms hanging down by her side.

'Why don't you speak out? What's the trouble? Has she been bullying you again?'

The servant shrugged her shoulders almost imperceptibly. Her old, wrinkled face was puffed with crying and, with the starched white apron tied over her belly that sagged from many childbirths, the white cap on her hair, she looked as

if her tired, work-worn body had donned a disguise for
fun.

'Sit down, Bozsi dear,' said Flora.

The woman remained standing.

'Sit down, I beg you,' the young painter repeated with a
nervous laugh. 'I'll drop dead with nervousness this very
minute if you don't sit down. Do I have to go down on my
knees?'

She lit a cigarette, blew out a cloud of smoke, and waited.
Sooner or later she would start talking! Quick, shiny tears
dripped down the sides of the servant's nose onto the apron
which was already dotted with small, wet spots. The veins
of her hanging hands stood out blue.

'Well?'

'I can't stand it any longer, Fairy Princess,' the woman said.

The young artist burst out laughing.

'One can stand anything. What is it you can't stand?'

'She won't let him die,' the servant said in a dull voice.

'She won't let him die?'

'She won't.'

'Good for her,' said Flora swallowing deeply. 'Good for her.'

The servant turned away. Flora watched her shoulders. She
had to be careful lest her eyes, too, fill with tears. 'It's natural
that she should do everything to keep him alive,' she said.
'Wouldn't you do the same? Tell me that if he were your
husband, wouldn't you do the same? For God's sake, open
that frozen mouth of yours or I'll jump out of my skin. Your
back is shaking, am I supposed to know what that means?
Why don't you speak? Wouldn't you do the same if your
husband were ill?'

'No,' said the servant in a low voice, leaning her back
against the dresser.

The girl dropped her cigarette on the floor and crushed it
with her foot.

'Murderer,' she said. 'Monster. Wicked female. Vicious poisoner. You would do the same.'

'No,' said the servant.

'And why not?'

The servant made no reply. Only her broad back was visible, she did not show her face.

'You won't talk, you won't talk!' the young painter cried desperately, kicking her crushed cigarette butt viciously under the dresser. 'I asked you why not?'

'Because I loved my husband,' the servant said.

The girl did not reply immediately. Her throat contracted.

'You listen here!' she said. 'You listen here! Comb my hair, God bless you. There's such a wind that my hair is all over the place, I daren't go in like this. Do comb my hair, angel, will you? No one in the world can put my hair up as you can.'

She shook her head. The hairpins rattled to the floor, the coal-black shiny knot of hair fell apart, and cascaded down to her waist. The servant turned, wiped her eyes with her apron and threw a quick glance at the slender girl in her white piqué frock. The sun, streaming in through the kitchen window, fell straight on her, sucked all light from the white dress, only the girl's two small breasts remained in shadow and the shapely, darkening, tightly closed thighs under her skirt. When she lifted her round, white arms to her hair, two small, dark spots of sweat showed in her armpits. 'Come on, come on!' she said impatiently and her face, that blinked with its every atom in the strong sunlight, crumpled in a funny-sweet grimace.

'What are we waiting for? I'll grow old before you catch up with me on those two waddling feet of yours!'

She ran into the narrow maid's room and sat down on the bed.

'I'm coming, Fairy Princess,' said the servant.

'So she won't let him die?'

The comb sizzled and sparkled in the thick, black hair. In
a square, dull mirror at the foot of the bed, she could see the
servant's face. Flora knew that as was a habit of ageing
women, Bozsi was in love with her, and that she would calm
down if permitted to play with her hair. She reached back
and stroked the servant's arm.

'Well, and what's the trouble?'

'She's giving him caffeine and vitamins,' the woman said,
'instead of morphine.'

From the kitchen they could hear the low whistle of the
small espresso machine.

'I know,' the woman said, 'because she sends me to the
doctor for the prescriptions. The Master is in such pain that
he screams but they have no mercy on him.'

The painter closed her eyes for a moment.

'But if the doctor himself gives the prescriptions!'

'The doctor says that he shouldn't be given anything but
morphine,' the woman said quietly. 'Yesterday he refused to
give me caffeine but Madam telephoned him then sent me
back for the prescription.'

'So he did let you have it.'

'Yes,' the servant said and Flora saw in the mirror that
her eyes were again brimming with tears. 'If he didn't she
would go around telling people that he had killed the Master.'

'How long has this been going on?' the young girl asked.

'Two weeks.'

'Two weeks already?'

The woman in the mirror nodded.

'That's when the doctor first said that it was time to help
him die. Morphine, he said, only morphine, morphine, morphine, morphine.'

'Why are you blubbering again?'

'You're crying too, little Princess!'

The young girl jumped up. 'Because you are pulling my hair with that stupid comb,' she cried, beside herself, her eyes full of tears. 'You old witch, you'll wait long enough before I put up with your comb again! You've pulled out half my hair because your mind is always on something else, not your work!'

The servant looked at her thoughtfully for a moment, then she embraced the slender girl. 'Talk to her, Fairy Princess,' she entreated. 'You are the only one she might listen to. Tell her to let him die! Not to make him take baths! Not to force him to celebrate his birthday in a week's time! Not to compel him to dictate to the typist! There's nothing left in his body but pain.'

'Birthday celebration?' asked the girl.

'Madam has invited about forty people to it,' the servant said. 'But today, when I took him his lunch and he immediately brought it up again, the Master grasped my hand and said in a low voice, so that no one heard it but me: "Bozsi, let me die! I'll leave you a thousand *forints* in my will if you let me die!"'

The young painter sat back on the narrow bed.

'He's so weak, poor thing, that he dirties his bed like a child,' the woman said. 'It's no use my telling him that it's our fault, we are too wicked, too lazy not to be there in time, he's ashamed. Last night he rose and without calling anyone, he crept out of the room but he only got as far as the corridor. Then he collapsed. I carried him back in my arms because he is as light as a four-year-old. And now she torments him with his will.'

'Was it the lawyer who came in with me?' the girl asked from between her hands which she had clapped over her face.

'The notary.'

A bell rang in the kitchen. The servant waited until it

stopped jangling, then she took off her white apron, her white cap, and threw them on the floor. Her dark-grey dress was threadbare, the hem of the skirt was patched with a different material.

'I am not going in,' she said. 'Tell her, Fairy Princess, that I am not coming in, she can stop ringing for me. If the master wants me, I'll come. While he still lives I'll stay but Madam can stop ringing, because I won't go in.'

By the time Flora entered the room, the notary had gone. Mrs. V. sat in the living-room by the telephone.

'Hallo, is that the Academy Secretariat? Can I speak to Comrade Moldovan? . . . Hallo . . . F . . . F . . . Feri, dear, you couldn't do that to me, could you—go and bury Ödön at Rakoskereszttur? I insist on the Kerepes Cemetery ! . . . No, he isn't dead yet, thank God, but when the catastrophe does occur ! You cannot shame me by burying him at Rakoskereszttur, like a dog ! Well, who am I to speak to? The Democratic Women? Or perhaps the Federation of Scientific Institutes? You say I should speak to the Party? I don't know anyone at Agitprop. Who else can I turn to? Everyone abandons me, everyone abandons me, I have to see to everything alone, I have no more strength left, no, I can't stand it any longer . . .'

'Flora, wait a second !' she said to the girl who was crossing the room, covering the receiver with her palm. 'I want to talk to you.'

The girl walked on without replying. Mrs. V. dropped the receiver on the table and ran after the young painter. 'Ask him about the contents of his will !' she whispered excitedly. 'First of all, how much money there is in the bank, and whether he hasn't a savings account somewhere else. I'll leave you alone with him, perhaps he'll tell you.'

*   *   *

Leaning on the pillows stacked high at his back V. turned his eyes to the opening door. For a moment, the girl stood rooted to the threshold. She hadn't seen V. for five or six days. The man in the bed was a stranger.

The blinds were loosely lowered, only the twilight seeping in between the slats retrieved the room from darkness. On the table beside the bed burned a tiny, blue, nightlight. The bed was covered with books, books lay on the carpet, books were piled high on the bedside table. An indefinable, sweetish, nauseating smell of sickness hovered in the air. The neck of a glass urinal protruded from under the bed.

V. was covered up to the neck, he had his arms as well under the light coverlet. On the blanket where, above the sunken loins, one thought to detect the man's belly, a big grey cat sat, turning its yellow eyes towards the door as it opened, then closed. As the light, thick blanket concealed the outlines of the patient's body, only the two little hillocks over the feet betrayed its presence; the head itself lived an apparently independent life on the high, white pillows.

Death, which had advanced to the forehead and temples, gave the head an extraordinary significance though even during life it must have attracted one's gaze. Now only the bone structure was left, flesh and fat had melted away, the skin stuck to the bones. As the lower part of the face had become very thin it seemed, as if the naturally high, domed forehead had grown to twice its size and the two grey eyes, from under which all fatty tissues had disappeared, protruded slightly from their sockets. Their gaze had become strangely rigid and heavy. The lips were cracked, the ears had turned yellow, the cheeks were a dull grey. The whole large bone-face stared indifferently at the white wall opposite.

'Who is that?' asked the sick man, turning his eyes toward the door.

Flora did not reply immediately. The two grey eyes stared

at her for a while without seeing. The once wide jaw had become pointed, the nose sharp, like a blade.

'I don't want anyone to come in,' the man said. 'I want to be alone.'

'It's me, Uncle Ödön,' the girl whispered.

The protruding grey eyes went on staring but the young woman felt that they had not yet become aware of her. Her voice, however, had reached the cortex of the brain.

'Is it you, Flora?' the sick man whispered.

She took two steps, her legs would carry her no further. She stopped. 'It's me, Uncle Ödön,' she said.

Now the eyes caught sight of her. V.'s face came alive and, as if the bone structure of the head were attempting to imitate the once so gentle movements of the face, it pulled the lips wider and sketched a slow smile. 'Come closer,' the sick man said. 'Sit down by me, if you have a little time. Give me a few minutes. I am much better today.'

The distance between the head and the outlined feet appeared much shorter than the space the tall male body had once cut out for itself. The young girl's heart beat loudly. So one shrinks in death!

'I'm coming, Uncle Ödön,' she said. 'It's a bit dark in this room, I can hardly see.'

The sick man nodded. 'Yes, it is a bit dark. Sit down, please, make yourself comfortable. May I ask you to move that armchair a little so that I can see you face on? That's it. Thank you. With most visitors it's enough if I have the profile. I'd like to cover your knees with a plaid.'

'But it's warm, Uncle Ödön.'

V. did not reply immediately. 'I thought it was cold,' he said after a while. 'Is it warm outside as well?'

The young painter sat down in the armchair. 'Yes. A warm summer evening.'

'Is it evening already?'

'Not quite,' Flora said. 'Only dusk.'

V. nodded again. 'Later I shall ask you to pull up the blinds. Just now, I want you to rest. Are you tired?'

'Why should I be tired, Uncle Ödön?'

'Of course,' the sick man said. 'Why should you be tired? I am much better today too. Are you sure you aren't tired?'

'Quite sure.'

'Then, why aren't you laughing?'

To that the girl had no answer.

'I am used to hearing your laughter precede you,' the sick man said. 'I cannot see you yet, but I hear you laughing in the next room. I hear your bright, sweet, laughter. Preserve that as long as you can. As long as you can laugh, the ground won't slip from under your feet.'

'Of course,' the girl said.

'Are you surprised that I should be so talkative today!' the sick man asked smiling again. 'I feel much better today. I don't want to alarm you but you probably know yourself that this is usual a day or two before one dies.'

He fell silent and observed the girl who sat narrow and motionless in her white frock.

'Thank you,' he continued after a while, 'for not tiring me with protests. Just now I am perfectly happy and contented. This is the happiness of the accomplished, my dear, and I should not like to be disturbed in it. You are the only one I can tolerate now. How did you know that this was the time to come?'

The girl raised her head and looked the sick man in the eyes.

'I did not know,' she said. 'But I know that I shall never leave you again as long as ...'

The sick man smiled, waited.

'As long as you need me,' the girl said bravely, loudly.

'Fine,' the sick man nodded, 'fine. But you, little girl, will walk out of this room and leave the apartment the moment this euphoric state of mine ceases and my pains start up again which will inevitably happen in two or three hours. This is my wish.'

He looked at the girl with his slightly protruding eyes and gave her another smile.

'. . . This is my last wish,' he added in a low voice. 'Please, light a cigarette.'

'Don't you mind the smoke?' the girl asked.

'Come closer!' the sick man said. 'Please, blow the smoke on me. Smoke from your lips . . . it's almost as if you took my hand.'

The girl immediately extended both her hands towards the sick man.

'No,' he said slowly, tiredly. 'Don't take my hand. I cannot take it from under the blanket, nor do I want to. Let everything be as it is. I don't wish to rob eternity.'

The young painter turned her head away slightly. The two old grey eyes opposite gazed at her as openly, as hungrily, as an animal might look at food, straight, without pretence, with the tautness of vitality. The girl felt herself blushing but she hoped that it was not visible in the twilight. She shook her head stubbornly and turned back to the sick man.

'I have another request,' the latter said quietly. 'Give me a mirror, no matter how small. Here they hide all the mirrors from me.'

The girl opened her purse with shaking hands.

'It doesn't matter if it has powder on it,' the sick man said. 'On the contrary, all the better. Now turn away please.'

For a while he gazed at himself, raising the small, square mirror above his face, then moving it to the right and to the left of his head, then he put his hand back under the blanket holding on convulsively to the little mirror. Two veins pulsated furiously on both sides of his neck.

'So that's what has become of me,' he said simply.

The young painter turned back to him quickly.

'Sweet!' she said, 'my sweet! You are terrifyingly beauti-ful now. I have never seen anything more moving, more beautiful.'

'Be quiet!'   ,

The small silver wrist-watch hanging from a nail on the wall pointed to six fifteen. With a thin, metallic ticking it swallowed time that now would suddenly shrink, now again expand miles beyond the walls of the room. The young girl felt dizzy.

'Forgive me,' the sick man said, 'I seem to have taken advantage of my position. Yet, at this moment I feel so per-fectly well that I have no right to any breach of discipline. Not even if we take into account my ridiculous future. How-ever, the mirror frightened me a bit.'

'Darling,' the girl said.

V. fixed her again with his frank, demanding gaze.

'I know that you forgive me,' he said. 'That is why I shouldn't . . . Still, I'd like to ask you now to open all the windows. Pull up the blinds! I want to say good-bye to the gardens as well.'

The red light of the setting sun came suddenly streaming in through the window and the wide-open French door of the terrace. The sick man turned his face slowly, curiously, towards the garden. From his bed he could look out, between two spruces, onto the sunny slopes of Gugger Hill, and, to the right, the lower ridge of the Hill of Roses with its many villas. From the corner window on the other side which—as there was no danger of draught—Flora had also opened, one could see the long range of Mount Liberty topped by Mount Janos and below it, the small upthrust of Hunyad Peak.

'Man is a giant to be able to exclude all this at any time

with a wall, a blind,' the sick man said after a while. 'And how stupid man is not to realize that he is really excluding himself. Isn't it so?'

The young girl didn't dare answer: lifting his head slightly from the pillows. V. was so engrossed in his contemplation of the garden that he seemed to have forgotten his guest. It was the same hungry, straight, undisguised look which, before, he had buried in her eyes. His neck, the radius of which was now fully exposed, was disproportionately thin under the large head, like that of dolls moulded from dough and stuck with a toothpick to the body. On the two sides the two nodding muscles stood out under the skin.

'I have spent thirty years of my life here,' he said.

The girl stood by the window and looked at Gugger Hill.

'Thirty years,' the sick man repeated.

The young painter was twenty-two years old. He had been living here, among these trees, eight years already when she was born.

'Why don't you answer?' he asked.

'I am answering,' the girl said.

'Isn't it a lot?'

'What?'

'Thirty years.'

'Thirty years,' the girl said musingly, wiping a tear from the corner of her eye with the point of her index finger. 'No, it isn't a lot.'

'Of course, it is,' V. said. 'And I haven't even had a child in those thirty years.'

The young painter took hold of herself, turned away from the window and sat back next to the bed. 'You leave something else to posterity.'

The sick man was looking out of the window, his neck tensed. 'I am not complaining.'

'It wouldn't suit you if you did,' the girl said.

'I am not complaining,' V. repeated with sunny Gugger Hill and the Hill of Roses reflected in his eyes. 'I am preparing a balance sheet with all the objectivity that is obligatory on the edge of the grave.'

'Lie back on your pillow, my sweet,' said the girl.

V. did not hear her. 'Do you see that pale-green one-storey house up there, on the hill-side? There's a yellow house next to it with a red roof and a gable-window. It is the third house down from the edge of the forest. There is a small orchard in front of it with a high stone wall, but that doesn't belong to it. It was built the year I graduated from the university and moved here with my parents. Can you see it?'

'I see it,' the girl said.

V. kept his eyes fixed on the hill-side.

'For thirty years that ochre colour next to the pale-green has been annoying me. How can one be happy with a petty nature like mine? Should I have gone up there and repainted it myself? At times I dreamed that I went up, rang the bell, and very politely ... You understand?'

'I understand.'

'I buried my mother from here,' the sick man said after a while. 'In July. The garden was full of blackbirds. Just as it is now. There was one we named Marie and it answered to its name. In the winter of 1934 it disappeared. Perhaps it froze to death.'

'That's the year I was born,' said the girl.

'Have you never noticed,' said V. looking out into the garden, his neck tensed, 'how very few dead birds one sees? They disappear without trace. They are light, light ... Perhaps that's how man too should ... My mother died in this room.'

'Was she a beautiful woman?'

'Six months later I buried my father,' the sick man said. 'Yes, she was beautiful. My father was a gnome. His friends made fun of him and called him Tom Thumb. My mother adored him, I loathed and despised him. It was only when he died that I understood he was my father.'

'Lie back on the pillow,' the girl said. 'You can see the garden just as well from there.'

The sick man nodded. 'In a minute. This is an obligatory tribute to my dead. I have finished, there is no more. I didn't keep up with my relations and never had any friends. I was thrifty with my emotions as befits a man engaged in serious work. Because I've worked all my life.'

The girl rose and bent over him.

'I beg you, lie back.'

'In a moment,' the sick man said. 'I've worked all my life. Please, sit down. Don't worry about me, my dear, I am perfectly well and unbelievably strong. You see, as long as this cat sits on my lap with its velvety-warm body, I know that all is well. The moment it senses danger it will jump off the bed without once looking back. That is what I want from you as well, little girl.'

'Yes,' she said.

Slowly V. let his head fall back on the pillow. Again he stared in front of him, at the white wall opposite. The wall was bare, he wouldn't allow a single painting on its surface.

'It's too much,' said the sick man staring at the wall. 'All the superfluous effort.' The cat rolled its yellow eyes towards the young painter and began to purr.

'Why don't you answer?' the sick man asked after a while.

'What did you say, my sweet?'

'It is too much!'

'It isn't,' the girl said.

'It is. You know what I mean.'

'Thirty years.'

'Yes,' said the sick man. 'Thirty years. It is too much.'

The girl shook her head violently. 'No, it isn't too much. I know now that I would give half my life if I had thirty years to . . .'

'Careful, my dear, don't shake your head, you'll spoil your hair,' the sick man said. 'It is too much. To sit for another thirty years under the walnut tree and look at . . . What do you call that hill?'

The girl followed the sick man's gaze.

'Liberty Hill.'

'You see?' the sick man said with satisfaction. He gave the girl a mocking look and broke into a smile. 'And I call it Swabian Hill. What business has a generation on this earth which still calls Liberty Hill Swabian Hill? Shall I myself survive my words, my system of symbols? What business has a man, who calls Liberty Hill Swabian Hill, with you? Yes, with you, with you in the first place! No, no, no! Thirty years. Too much! I don't want to sit under the walnut tree any longer.'

The young girl looked in alarm at the suddenly distorted face. The big, bald skull was dry but beads of sweat shone on the forehead and temples. She threw herself down on her knees and buried her head in the blanket.

'Sit back,' the sick man said. 'There's nothing the matter with me, I'm perfectly all right. Pardon my outburst. Bad form. Will you forgive me?'

The young painter rose and sat back in the armchair.

'Fix your hair,' said the sick man. 'I should like to throw this rug over your knees. Are you sure you are not cold?'

The girl shook her head.

'All right,' the sick man said. 'Of course. It is a warm summer evening. Give me a little champagne, please, I am thirsty. Turn away or, better, go to the window for a moment.

I don't want you to see my hand. There's a glass on the table here, pour it in.'

He lifted the glass carefully, imbibed half a mouthful, rinsed out his palate and tongue, then spat the liquid back into the white china bowl on his bed. He himself replaced the glass on the table. The effort tired him out. 'Come back, little girl,' he said in a low voice. 'It's safe for you to stay a bit longer if you have the time, I'll let you know . . . Unfortunately, the body is immodest.'

The young painter sat back in the armchair.

'It steps beyond itself,' the sick man said quietly. 'It wants to expand in time as well as in space, in a medium alien to it. Stay where you are, stay in your place—I should like to tell it, once I've done my final accounts and settled all my affairs—but no, it goes on writhing, prancing, veritably yearning for eternity. Ridiculous pretentiousness!'

'Have you done your accounts?' the young painter asked.

'Ridiculous pretentiousness,' the sick man repeated, 'just as if it were raising its arms and trying to reach the stars. The stars. What do you say to that? Instead of making itself small, assuming the correct proportions allotted to it in space and time and, when the time to shrink arrives, returning slowly, without protest, even willingly, into the dust. But no! . . . the stars!'

The young painter lowered her eyes.

'Yes, I have done my accounts,' the sick man said. 'And now it would befit this body to wait for death like an old man who has lost all his teeth and nourishes himself once a day with a little bread soaked in coffee . . .'

'But you still have teeth!' the girl whispered, her eyes downcast.

'No,' the sick man said.

A thrush was warbling in the garden. A mild little breeze

drifted in through the open French door opposite the sick man's bed, which looked out on a dark green lawn bordered with flowerbeds, setting the lace curtains that had been drawn aside, aflutter.

'No,' the sick man said irritably, 'It's a delusion, self-deception, one of the body's old, cunning tricks. A while ago, when you entered the room and I heard your voice but hadn't yet seen you . . .'

'Did you really not see me?'

The sick man didn't reply immediately. 'Forget it!' he said with a tired smile after a short deliberation. 'I am trying to fool you, too? Not only myself? . . . Suddenly you were standing before me, a few steps away, white, slender, with your raven-black hair, holding out your two arms towards me like a vision, and attracting to yourself all the light there was in the room. Obviously this was a conspiracy of beauty and desire designed to make me live on. To the stars! The stars! . . . Well, no. As I said before, I've done my last accounts.'

'Really?' the girl asked in a low voice, her eyes downcast. 'In that case why did you ask me to pull up the blinds?'

The sick man looked at her. 'You are cruel,' he said.

He turned away his head and gazed out into the garden. The sun had retreated from the lawn and now rose slowly away from the earth, climbing the branches of the two spruces standing by the fence. Thrushes warbled. The flowerbeds round the lawn which had sunk into shadow, began to emit a stronger fragrance. Above the setting sun, long strips of cloud threw a red, glowing, velvety light.

'Gorgeous sunset,' the sick man said. 'I know it, I know it far too well. But there is a time for birth and a time for death, a time for sowing and a time for reaping what has been sown . . . It can't fool me any longer. Are you aware of my condition?'

'Yes,' the girl said.

V. broke into a smile and it seemed to the girl as if a cruel gleam flashed in the tired, old eyes.

'You don't. If it doesn't disgust you I shall describe it in a few brief words. In my foolish youth I acquired a medical degree as well, so I have some inkling of that profession. You know that I have cancer?'

'Let's not talk about it,' said the girl turning white.

'If you think I must be spared,' the sick man continued, 'allow me to go on speaking. You can do so without risk as, I told you, I have long ago made my last accounts. A short while ago I was given a novocaine block and I feel perfectly well, my dear. Besides, it won't take long. You also know that I am beyond operation. The surgeons cut me open and promptly sewed me up again.'

'Please stop I beg of you!' the girl said. 'Stop!'

The sick man looked at her with his slightly protruding eyes. 'Are you frightened? What of?'

'I am not frightened.'

'Courage, little girl!' the sick man said. 'When you entered this room you probably knew this would be our last conversation. You didn't know? Don't lie to me!'

The girl shook her head. 'I am not lying.'

'Morphine, which is going to help me through my last hours,' the sick man went on, 'limits the functioning of the central nervous system; novocaine, on the other hand, acts locally, so one remains absolutely lucid. A short while ago I received one of the above mentioned novocaine blocks against the pain in my back which comes, presumably, from a metastasis to the vertebrae, and it completely stopped the pain without in any way impairing the functioning of the cerebral cortex. I can see very clearly, my dear. One of the conditions of happiness, or rather, what we call happiness, is that we should understand ourselves.'

'I understand,' said the girl.

The sick man nodded. 'Right,' he said. His voice sounded weaker but he obviously didn't notice. 'Right. The blood, or the lymph circulation has scattered the cancerous cells throughout the organism. In addition to the spine, they have, it can be assumed, attacked also the pancreas and the liver, presumably my lungs as well, because I've been coughing since yesterday. The swelling that has developed on the abdominal wall is the size of your fist and as hard as a board; it can be detected with the fingers in all its circumference.'

'Stop!' the girl cried beside herself. 'How long do you want to go on tormenting me?'

'One more minute,' said the sick man breathing laboriously. 'Your little powdery mirror that I am holding in my hand under the blanket has most reassuringly justified everything I have said about the rapid spread of metastases. Dry, wrinkled skin, a dull, greyish-yellow colour, pointed chin, sharp nose. Protruding, dilated eyes. Wax-yellow ears, neck muscles in relief. An old, apathetic face. If, to this, I add the jutting-out ribs, hip-bones that have become prominent, the emaciated match-stick legs, you have the complete clinical picture of carcinoma. And now, up to the stars!'

The young painter looked at him with such desperate eyes that the sick man took pity on her.

'Calm yourself, Flora,' he said, 'all I wanted to do was to illustrate to you what I said about the body's pretentiousness. Or the soul's, if you prefer it. I have brought to an end in myself all that had to be brought to an end, but the senseless matter goes on working and struggling. And that's how it's been all through my life. I was always greedy and immodest.'

'Now I want to ask you something,' said the girl in a determined voice casting a look of almost undisguised anger

at the bone-face lying on the pillow. 'Don't try to detract
from your life, you have no right to do that. Your life
was not only yours, you cannot pass judgment on it
alone.'

'Do you believe that?' the sick man asked; as if blinded by
the purple colours of the sunset, he closed his eyes for a
moment. 'Do you believe that?'

'I know it,' the girl said and her tiny hands bunched involuntarily into fists. There, next to the dying man's bed, the
infinite self-confidence of her slender young body was a cruel
challenge.

'There you are!' said the sick man. 'She would defend my
life even against me. In whose name? Obviously in mankind's.'

'Yes,' said the girl.

The sick man lay silent, watching the pale, young face.
'You see only the surface, child. Apparently it is more than
the whole if it is able to call forth such enthusiasm. Do you
not want to look any deeper?'

'Who could see past your achievements?' said the girl.

The room was quiet again.

'Apparently there is no medicine against faith,' said the
sick man excitedly, breathing more rapidly. 'Faith leads the
war and behind it comes its shadow; self-deception. Is that
what my work taught you? My achievements are insignificant compared with the suffering I have caused myself and
society. Look around in my environment: whom have I
made happy? Is there a single man? A single woman? An
indication of immeasurable ambition: I always despised the
present. I deluded myself that I was living for the future. The
future! The stars! What children did they bear me? Doubt-
ful achievements that won't even live out an average life-
span.'

'How do you know that your descendants would have lived

to an older age?' the girl asked, grasping the arms of her chair in her excitement.

The sick man ignored the question. 'My entire life is a cancerous overgrowth of the future,' he said. 'I have never thought of myself, only of my achievements. I never cared whether or not I was feeling contented, all I cared about was whether or not my work was going well. I exchanged every minute of the present for a promise. Do you think that, when I was sitting under the walnut tree, I heard the birds singing? In half an hour I'd forgotten what I had for lunch. I never knew when it was time to put on clean underwear. I lied to myself that I had something more important to do. I lied to myself ceaselessly, all my life.'

'It isn't true,' the girl said, very pale.

The sick man paid no attention to her. He looked at the white wall opposite his bed which seemed to calm him down a little with its finite proportions. 'In people of my sort,' he said, 'one can frequently observe this pathological overgrowth of the future. They are not satisfied with the modest future which is contained in every present act and which would develop their lives naturally, at a nice tempo. No, they want more, they want much, at least one hundred years, or better still, eternity. They do not listen to their natural leanings that could warn them in time, before they turned into drug addicts of the future. They eat, they devour the present, the only reality. They lie to themselves that they are serving mankind. Gradually every moment, every movement becomes a lie. And, if they lie to themselves, what could be more natural than that they should lie to others as well. They lie, lie, endlessly.'

'Aren't you thirsty?' asked the girl loudly to attract his attention. 'Shall I pour you out a little champagne?'

'What I ask of you,' the sick man said, 'is never to make common cause with people who lack a sense of proportion.

Don't ever tie your future to them, give them a wide berth.
They are the wolves of their environment. The wolves of
mankind.'

The girl lowered her eyes and kept silent.

'Can't you hear me?' the sick man asked. 'Is my voice too
low?'

'I can hear you,' the girl said.

'Then why don't you answer?'

'I'm afraid of tiring you out,' said the girl.

'I am not tired.'

The girl pulled her chair closer to the bed. 'That's good,'
she said. 'Then let's be quiet for a little while.'

'I am not tired,' the sick man repeated. 'Why don't you
answer me?'

'Sweet one,' the girl said, 'Let's be quiet for a little while
now.'

The sick man shook his head almost impeceptibly. 'And
what if I were tired!' he said. 'This is our last conversation.'

'I'll shut the windows,' the girl said, 'the sun has gone
down. It gets cool very rapidly at this hour.'

The eyes of the sick man followed her light stride to the
window, her arms rising to the latch, her wavering, alarmed,
path back to the bed.

'Have I tired you out, Flora?' he asked.

The girl smiled at him without answering.

'Have I frightened you?'

'You only scared me,' the girl said. 'I feel so helpless.'

'Do you want to go?'

'Never!' the girl cried. 'Never!'

The sick man looked at her, his tired, dull gaze clung
expressionlessly to her face.

'Why do you feel helpless?'

'Because I cannot . . .'

'Comfort me?' the sick man asked after waiting, in vain, for her to continue. His voice was so hoarse now that the girl bent involuntarily closer.

'No,' she replied quickly, in a determined voice, shaking her head angrily. 'Not comfort you, that's something you don't need, but to find proof.'

'Proof that I am wrong?'

'Yes,' the girl said. 'Yes.'

The sick man sighed, for the first time in the course of their conversation. 'I know,' he said. 'There is no remedy against faith, that's why people like me succeed. Our lies survive us.'

'Not your lies,' the girl said, 'but your truths.'

The sick man sighed again. He turned away his head and glanced at the bottle of champagne standing on the bedside table.

'There is only a little left in the bottle,' the girl said.

'It doesn't matter.'

'Will half a glass be enough?'

'Yes. You don't have to turn away.'

She remained standing by the bed. The sick man rinsed out his mouth then spat the liquid back into the bowl. He watched the girl from the corner of his eye. He had to cough, he could not suppress it. He took another mouthful of champagne. When he lay back on the pillow he felt the blood rising to his head.

'Would you take my hand?' he asked after a while.

The young girl's eyes filled with tears.

'Warm it a little!' the sick man said. 'It seems to be a cool evening.'

'Yes, it is cool. I should have closed the windows before.'

Enraptured, the sick man stared at the two slim, white, young hands that encompassed his bones with their smooth softness.

'The evenings are always cool out here.'

'Yes, they are cool,' the girl said.

'Even in the hottest summer.'

'Yes, even then,' the girl said. 'One feels cold sometimes even in August.'

'I noticed too late that I had become a stranger among men,' the sick man said. His voice faltered, he drew a deep breath between words. The girl had to bend still closer to understand him. 'Once, that was a few years ago, some children pelted me while I was out walking.'

'With snow?'

'Yes.'

'Why?' asked the girl.

'Because I was a stranger among men.'

The girl squeezed the cold hand.

'You didn't know them?'

'No,' the sick man said. 'They were screeching and playing in the snow. Up here, on the hill. I was coming along in the middle of the road, with slow, dignified steps, alone, in a black overcoat, with a black fur-cap on my head, dark sunglasses, filled with the knowledge of my superiority. For a while they watched me, then they began to pelt me. There must have been ten or fifteen of them. They made a ring round me, threw snow-balls at me, my eyes, my mouth, were full of snow. As if I had been some strange animal. They didn't discuss it among themselves, they just flew at me. As if I had been an animal. And yet, I hadn't done anything to them.'

'And you can't forget it,' the girl said and her heart contracted with pity.

'No,' the sick man said.

The girl again squeezed his hand. 'Sweet one. Poor sweet.'

'They kept on at it for a long time,' the sick man said.

'What could I have done? If I'd shouted at them, they'd have laughed because they knew that if they ran I couldn't catch them. Had I tried to run away they would have pursued me. I just stood there, motionless, and they pelted me with snowballs with compressed lips. For a long time.'

'And you didn't say a word?' the girl asked.

'Not a word,' the sick man said. 'I didn't know what to say.'

The young painter fought bravely with her tears. She lowered her head and stroked the sick man's hand.

'And now you must go, little girl,' the sick man said suddenly.

'Already?'

'Let go of my hand!'

'Let me stay a little longer!' the girl said.

The sick man coughed. 'You must go.'

'I can't,' the girl said, her eyes filled with tears. 'Don't consider me.'

'You upset me,' the sick man said. His voice was hoarse, his breath whistled. 'You know what you promised.'

'Yes.'

'You must go now. You upset me. Do you hear me?'

'Yes.'

'Do you hear what I say?'

'I hear you, sweet.'

'All right,' the sick man said. 'I have another request.'

'Yes.'

'Do you hear me?'

The girl nodded. 'Yes.'

'Don't be hard on my wife!' the sick man said. 'Whatever the poor thing does.'

'Yes,' said the girl.

'Thank you. And now lower the blinds and go!'

'Yes.'

'A sense of proportion,' the sick man said falteringly. 'A sense of proportion. You won't forget?'

The girl shook her head. 'No.'

'If you don't forget, I shall die in peace.'

'I won't forget,' the girl said.

The sick man closed his eyes. 'Lower the blinds and go!' he said.

The young girl knelt down by the bed and kissed the sick man's hand. She kissed it for a long time and pressed her soft face to it. Tears flowed from her eyes.

'Good-bye, my love,' the sick man whispered.

The girl rose, lowered the blinds, the room was darkened, she went out through the door.

*   *   *

'Take a piece of paper and write down all the pet names he called me by!' the woman instructed the servant, freshening her swollen, tear-reddened face with a wad of cotton wool soaked in eau de Cologne. 'Write down everything you can remember! Write it in the household accounts book, you'll only lose a piece of paper. What do you remember?'

The three old women were weeping, sniffing, wiping their tears. Apart from them, the elderly, grey-haired man sat in his usual place in the brocade armchair holding a book close to his eyes and engrossed in his reading; there was no one else in the room. 'What pet-names can you recall?' the woman asked.

'Snubnose!' Aunt Matild said. 'He used to call you Snubnose.'

Mrs. V. took a mirror and carefully examined her little snub nose; it was badly swollen with weeping.

'What else?'

'Snubby,' said Aunt Roza. 'He also called you Snubby!'

'Can't you remember anything else?' the woman asked after a while.

'Sometimes he'd call you Sweetheart,' said Aunt Matild.

Aunt Roza wiped her eyes. 'My little Sweetheart.'

'Sweetie,' said Aunt Berta.

'Is that all?' the woman called nervously. 'But he simply drowned me in pet-names! In the condition I'm in, it is not surprising that I should forget everything, but you really should know . . .'

The grey-haired man reading in the armchair, rose, put the book back on the shelf, selected another and sat down again.

'That's all I remember,' said Aunt Matild.

Aunt Roza wiped her eyes. 'Snubby . . . Snubby darling . . .'

In her agitation the woman overturned the bottle of eau-de-Cologne. 'Was that all?' she whispered to herself. 'They're taking everything from me, even his love! And my so-called friends are the first to desert me . . .'

'Calm down, my dear child,' said Aunt Matild. 'It is not the words that count.'

'There wasn't anybody in the whole world he loved so much, I'll vouch for that,' said Aunt Roza.

The woman looked expectantly at the third old woman, the shaky-headed Aunt Berta. The old lady's head shook more quickly, her forehead under the white hair was more than usually wrinkled from the exhausting brainwork.

'I've got it,' she cried triumphantly in her thin, slimy voice. 'These two, of course, remember nothing! He used to call you Bumblebee!'

'That was twenty years ago,' murmured Aunt Matild, careful that the woman should not hear her, and threw a contemptuous glance at Aunt Berta's shaking head. Aunt Roza nodded approvingly. 'What is going to become of me?' the woman mumbled, wiping her eyes.

The door of the death-chamber opened and the sculptor, who had been preparing a plaster cast of the dead man's hand, came up to the table.

'I couldn't stand it in there any longer,' the woman told him apologetically giving the sculptor a broken-hearted look from her beautiful, velvety-brown eyes. 'When you took his wrist and lifted that hand that once...'

At the woman's request, the visitors were sitting on the porch or in the garden so as 'not to disturb the dead man's last sleep'. The front door bell signalled the arrival of more and more guests whom the servant led out on to the porch, before announcing them to the lady of the house; from time to time, she would appear among them and hold out her hand or her cheek for a kiss, acknowledging their condolences with mute dignity, concealing her suffering heroically, or breaking into loud uncontrollable sobs. Every hour the postman would arrive with the telegrams which Aunt Matild read aloud to the woman and then placed in a large silver dish in the centre of the table like a collection of calling cards in the drawing room of heaven or hell.

'How many?' the widow asked.

'Thirty-one.'

'Impossible,' exclaimed the widow. 'There were thirty-two last time you counted them. Count them again!'

But Aunt Matild was so exhausted by the recent matter of pet-names that she blinked her tear-filled eyes and pushed the silver dish in front of Aunt Roza. The latter shook her head, sighed deeply, and did not touch it. They understood each other. Aunt Berta sat staring at the dish, her head shaking, her eyes hungry.

'Thirty-six,' she said. 'I remember, it was thirty-six.'

'You handle the telegrams,' the woman said. 'Make a list so that we know who to send notices of death to.'

'Yes, Berta, make a list!' said Aunt Matild triumphantly,

eyeing Aunt Roza slyly. The latter made an innocent face
and sighed. 'That's it, let her write it out,' she said contentedly.

As the sculptor had accomplished his task, the photographer, who had been called upon at the widow's wish to
take a last picture of V. could at last get to work. But no
sooner had the first cloud of magnesium smoke dispersed,
than the woman was called out from the death-chamber. An
official of the praesidium of the Patriotic People's Front, a
bent, tired-eyed elderly man, wished to speak to the widow
personally about the funeral.

'Good day, Comrade,' the woman said. 'Thank you for
coming, we have a great deal to discuss. Please, take a seat.
Have we got it?'

'Got what, Comrade?' the official asked.

'The Cemetery of Kerepes.'

'I should like to persuade you, Comrade . . .' the official
replied after a short obviously embarrassed pause, 'I should
like to persuade you . . .'

'To do what?' the widow rose from her chair.

'. . . to give up the idea . . .'

Mrs. V. changed colour. Her eyes rolled and dilated, her
nostrils grew livid. Like a post dug from its setting, she tilted,
then fell over rigidly. Fortunately she was warmly received
by the red davenport behind her, even the arm-rest yielded
to her widowed head. In a few minutes, the three black-clad
old women had tidied her up, raised her to a sitting position,
and quietened her insane screams that carried all the way to
the porch. Then they called to her side the nervously fidgeting official who had turned away modestly and who, in his
past career as an Ujpest Cabinetmaker, had garnered little
experience in the comforting of suffering widows.

'Will you please understand once and for all that it is not
up to us!' he said with suppressed anger. 'As far as I am

concerned, they can bury him under the Millenium Memorial,
I won't protest. And don't shout at me, I am not deaf!'

In the meantime, Aunt Matild had run out to the porch
for help and was now returning with the representative of
the Hungarian-Soviet Society, a pale, skinny, bespectacled
woman, an acquaintance of the V.s.

'Calm down, my dear, I'll take care of it,' she said. 'The
comrade and I will go at once to Party Headquarters and there
we shall personally discuss the problem with Comrade Lukacs.
I am convinced that the comrades will appreciate the situation . . .'

'The Municipal Funeral Enterprise has already been informed that he's being put in the Farkasret Cemetery . . .'
the official said.

The bespectacled woman nudged him with her elbow.
'We'll take care of that, Comrade.'

'I've had my orders from Comrade Bogati, Vice-President
of the EC . . .'

'All right, we'll take care of it . . .' the thin woman said.

The official mopped his perspiring brow. 'Too late. They
are coming for the body in an hour's time.'

The widow threw back her head. 'I won't let him go,' she
cried passionately, 'I won't let him go! You can't have him
before seven o'clock. His friends want to take leave of him,
everybody's coming in the afternoon . . .'

'All right, dear, we'll settle it.'

'A resident of Buda cannot be buried in Pest,' the official
said with stubborn innocence, 'that is laid down by law.'

'I won't allow him to be taken away,' the widow cried. 'No
one can enter this apartment unless I invite them in. By the
way, who is going to speak on behalf of the Patriotic People's
Front?'

The official shrugged but made no reply.

'You don't know? Who's speaking for your lot?' the

widow turned to the bespectacled woman. 'Don't you know
either?'

'No one's been selected yet, my dear,' the woman said.

The widow stared in front of her for a long time, her chin
pressed to her chest.

'Let me tell you right now, that I won't let just anybody
speak at the grave. Some people, of course, would like it, if
some upstart or other delivered the funeral oration, if possible,
someone who hated Ödön all his life. Well, they can think
again! I want to know who speaks. Who will be the Party's
speaker?'

'That will be decided later, my dear,' said the bespectacled
woman.

'They had better not send some minor official, I'd prefer
not to have him buried at all!' cried the widow. She felt that
she was nearing the end of her tether. 'When is the funeral
to be?'

'On Friday.'

'When?'

'The day after tomorrow, Friday.'

The widow was silent for a long time, amassing her remain-
ing forces. At the bottom of her heart she knew that she
would not survive her husband by long, nor did she much
desire it. She was mortally tired, she yearned for peace, quiet,
resignation. She dropped her head on the cushion. 'That is
out of the question,' she cried in a trembling voice. 'He will
be buried on Sunday.'

'Why?' asked the representative of the Hungarian-Soviet
Society, surprised. 'Why can't it be on Friday?'

'Because people have no time to go to funerals,' said the
widow with a last show of strength. 'At least two or three
hundred less would come on a Friday. Is this democracy? To
deprive the working people of their last chance to say good-
bye?'

'But my dear, there are no funerals on Sundays!' said the bespectacled woman.

The widow shut her eyes. 'Somlay was buried on a Sunday!'

'Sunday?'

'The funeral cannot be held on Sunday,' said the official of the Patriotic People's Front. 'It would cost at least 5,000 *forints* extra.'

'I can't bear it,' the widow sighed. 'I just can't bear it. Wasn't Ödön V. worth 5,000 *forints* to you?'

The servant came in to announce that the men from the funeral enterprise had arrived to collect the body.

*   *   *

By one o'clock on Friday, a hundred or a hundred and fifty people had assembled around V.'s bier in the Kerepes Cemetery. It was a cloudless summer day and although the barracks-like cemetery was doing its utmost to preserve in non-being, as in being, the symmetrical order of the human mentality and prevent the infiltration of the dead into the light, rapid circulation of matter, nature outwitted it with its own broadly understandable and subtle dignity; in unguarded moments the laurels growing luxuriantly behind the heavy headstones, or the roses, primroses and carnations flowering on the graves would naively blend and confuse the narrow notions of death and birth. In the hot sunshine, gay little breezes kept lifting the dust of decay from the souls. The avenue of tall poplars along which the crowd streamed towards the bier linked the earth with the sky. Here and there, the freshly gilded letters on a marble tomb-stone caught the fairy feet of dancing sun-rays and covered them with kisses. The short whistles of a locomotive called across the wall from the rail-network flanking the cemetery.

The news of the elegant funeral had brought out the habitués of the Kerepes Cemetery. Soon the professional old guard

of the graves were all there around the chapel of rest, praying
for the soul of the unknown dead and receiving with apprecia-
tive nods the rich wreaths arriving in large numbers. The long
lines of private cars and taxis advanced at walking pace along
the wide, freshly watered avenue between the hurrying
pedestrians. Now and again a visitor on his way home from
the cemetery would turn round at sight of the magnificent
procession and join the unknown mourners.

Those who could not enter the chapel to stand round the
coffin stood outside in long, dense rows. Because of the blinding sunshine, one could not see from out there what was happening in the dark black-draped room illuminated only by
the dim candles throwing flame-yellow spots onto the stiff
faces of the black-clad mourners. The wreaths were still arriving, the funeral service had not yet begun. The widow stood
at the head of the coffin, opposite the entrance; the candle
light fell on her face from which, in her agitation, she had
thrown back the black veil over the brim of her hat. Even
from outside she could be seen striking the lid of the closed
coffin with her fist.

'I demand that it be opened immediately,' she cried, so
loudly that those standing near the entrance could hear her.
'I want to see what you have done with him!'

The clerk of the funeral enterprise whispered in her ear,
wiping his red-boiled, sweating face.

'I don't care!' shouted the widow. 'Why didn't you put him
on ice? To save more money? At every funeral I've ever
attended, the coffin was always open. I demand that you have
it opened this instant!'

The clerk had two possible suspicions to dispel; one, that
the coffin was empty, two, that they had stolen the clothes
off the body. He made those standing close to the bier retreat
and asked the widow to step up on the platform. While bending forward for a better view into the coffin, under its lifted

lid, Mrs. V. overturned two candles; fortunately, both went
out while falling and caused no conflagration. When she
straightened up and stepped down from the platform, she
knocked over a third candle; this caused some alarm because
the candle fell among the black drapes, before it rolled under
the platform. Again, nothing happened, the fire was stamped
out in time.

'He isn't decaying yet,' said the widow to her sister on
whose arm she was leaning, 'but he's foaming at the mouth.'

The Party speaker began his oration. His voice was weak
and his words did not carry to the mourners lined up outside
the chapel, who strained their ears for a while, trying to hear,
then, exhausted by the vain effort, settled back among their
common, everyday worries. A long way back, one step behind
the last row of people, an elderly, grey-haired man stood reading, lifting his book close to his eyes.

'She telephoned me at seven o'clock in the morning,' the
editor of the banned neo-Catholic periodical, who had received eighty or a hundred *forints* assistance a month from
the deceased, informed his neighbour. "Ödön has just died in
my arms," she said, "come immediately!" Unfortunately, such
a feeling of exhaustion came over me at the news that I went
back to sleep and it was noon by the time I got there. You
can imagine the reproachful look . . .'

'In her arms? Not on your life!' whispered the daughter
of the deported criminologist who had been given fifty *forints*
a month and dinner every Sunday by the V.s. 'I know from
Aunt Matild who spent the night there that they didn't dare
go into the sickroom . . .'

'What happened?'

'They rang for the maid servant at six o'clock in the morning . . .'

In the row opposite stood the Countess who obtained one
hundred and twenty *forints* a month from Mrs. V.'s private

funds. Turning her eyes right and left, she watched her neighbours.

'Do you know,' she whispered to her neighbour, the wife of the imprisoned gynaecologist, who received two hundred *forints* a month from the V.s. 'Do you know that on the day before he died she telephoned all the lawyers they know to ask whether they didn't have a more recent will of his . . .'

'She went to the banks as well,' said the wife of the gynaecologist.

'What banks?'

'To all the branches of the National Savings Bank. By taxi. She had Ödön's photo with her and asked them whether they knew him . . .'

'They rang for the maid servant and sent her into the room to find out what was happening in there. Neither of them dared go in.'

'But why did they ring for her?'

'Aunt Matild was awakened by the cat mewing in the sick-room and scratching the door. She waited for a while, then wakened . . .'

'Wasn't the dying man making any noise? No death-rattle?'

'They heard nothing. Not even the poor man's breathing. So they rang for the maid because neither dared go in . . .'

The widow of the former president of the British-Hungarian Bank who got a hundred and fifty *forints* a month from the V.s, had just arrived, but a moment later she was wiping the sweat from her huge, red face in the first row. 'I just heard that this damned fool, this two-legged cow, who should be banned from the Continent, lest England declare war on us . . .'

'Why should England declare war on us, Your Ladyship?' asked the tabetic painter. 'In the name of offended human reason? Or in defence of human rights? To my knowledge,

this extremely attractive nation does not deny man his right
to stupidity.'

The fat widow pushed the short, thin painter back with
her elbow. 'I'm glad to see you. But why did you come out
here with your game leg? You'll never sell them another
picture anyway, my boy!'

'I'd like to do a portrait of you,' said the painter.

'You are another damned fool. Do you think I'll ever have a
blasted penny? Well, I hear that this . . .'

'She showed his picture at every branch of the Bank and
asked whether he didn't have a deposit.'

'And did they tell her?'

'Of course they didn't. Deposits are confidential, they are
not allowed to tell. They explained this to her at the first
branch she went to, nevertheless, she sat back in her taxi
and went on . . .'

'I hear she is looking for some Swiss shares that Ödön got
from her as her dowry.'

The solemn cadence of a strong, agreeable male voice was
heard from the mortuary but the speaker was obviously
standing with his back to the entrance because his words
were unintelligible. A reporter's bulb flashed, then another,
and a third.

'But by the time the maid went into the room he was dead.'

'How awful! Was he alone when he died?'

'Alone.'

'His wife was not with him?'

'Well he wouldn't be very put out about that, my dear
editor.'

'How malicious you are, Countess. God is my witness, you
are worse than I am.'

The Countess smiled delicately. 'It appears that he wished
to be alone in his last minutes. When the maid entered . . .'

'She took my last pair of nylons, poor thing,' the County

Lieutenant's widow informed those standing near her. 'I almost didn't come to the funeral because of it. Of course I can see that she needs them more . . .'

'Anyway, I hear that this two-legged cow asked the dying man to write something in her souvenir album before he died. The bloody fool! She's lucky we haven't met since, or . . .'

'Two days before his death she wanted to go to the theatre . . .'

'She's asked me for tickets to the first night . . .'

'And how offended she was when . . .'

'Do you think there's enough money left, to . . .'

'. . . to go on paying you the hundred and twenty a month?'

'. . . she put a volume of Dante in his hand and wanted him to be photographed with it.'

'On his death bed?'

'Yes. But they couldn't force his fingers apart.'

'. . . she gets only fifty a month!'

'Not for long!'

'. . . a pink Shantung silk frock, and she didn't want to have it dyed . . .'

Every time the photographer aimed at the bier, and at the speakers as they took their place at the coffin one after the other, the widow threw back the veil from her face and turned her tear-reddened eyes towards the lens. The heat in the mortuary was suffocating, a young girl fainted, and had to be led out into the open. Outside, the fresh wind would stir up little clouds of dust, mixing them with the perfume of flowers coming from distant graves.

'Will you speak later, at the grave, Professor?'

'Yes,' said the elderly, grey-haired man sliding the open book he was holding quickly into his coat pocket. 'Yes, at the grave. Unfortunately, I always have to deliver funeral orations when my friends die and that prevents me from enjoying the funeral.'

'She taxied along to all the branches of the National Savings Bank, she even went out to Pesterzsebet . . .'

'And the Swiss shares?'

'They couldn't have been there. When she saw that she wasn't getting anywhere, she told Ödön a lie, namely that all bankotes were to be stamped next week, so everything should be withdrawn from the bank . . .'

'Why does your ladyship adore nature?' said the painter. 'The carcinogen is also part of nature, do you adore that as well?'

'Was Mrs. R. receiving a regular monthly allowance?'

'So he wanted to be alone when he died.'

'Yes, the servant went into the room, it was so dark there that at first she didn't dare go any further. He must have put the night light out.'

'He still had enough strength?'

'He had a terrible strength. He'd pulled the quilt over his face so that no one should hear his agony. He wanted to die alone. With his two skeleton hands he pressed the quilt to his face on both sides, and held it there so convulsively that he tore the lining.'

When the procession set out towards the grave, the painter fell back unnoticed and, a little unsteady on his two jerky legs, went on a little constitutional walk through the large cemetery. As he emerged from among the elegant crypts and monuments and reached the poorer, neglected section, the ironical smile that had pulled up the corners of his mouth at reading the inscriptions, melted slowly from his face and in his eyes the outer landscape met, and merged, with the inner landscape; his hard, bony face softened, became dreamy, his eyes brightened and filled with tears. Leaning his back against the tumble-down tombstone over which a giant weeping willow sifted the rain of sunshine, he sat down on the ground. Once upon a time—before they both grew a tough skin—he had been V.'s best friend and now suddenly the old memories attacked his heart and weighed it down. Round about him everything was silent, only the sunshine, raining down ceaselessly, made the trunk of the ancient tree emit a cracking sound and a sleepy chirping was heard from its crown. On the nearest, sundrenched tombstone, a bottle-green lizard lay sunning its delicately articulated, cartilaginous body; holding its three-cornered reptile-head rigidly forward, its four tiny feet stuck to the hot stone, it imbibed, motionless, the joy of being alive. The air was so clear that one could see on its neck, under the thin skin, the pulsating of a vein. A little breeze roamed among the tombstones, dissolved a breath of rose perfume in the warm air and shook one of the hanging tendrils of the laurel, then, having done its work, it disappeared tracelessly behind the shadow of the nearest cross.

From behind one of the graves an old woman stepped out into the sunshine. When she caught sight of the man lying on the ground sobbing convulsively she stopped and threw him a pitying glance from her rheumy, old eyes. In her life she had seen many men weep, and yet she could still not pass them without a word.

'Don't take it so much to heart, Comrade,' she said. 'You see, I've been coming here to pray at the grave of my only son for forty years now, and I still get along somehow. True I have a daughter too, and a lovely grandchild.'

The painter turned round and wiped away his tears with his handkerchief. The old woman bent forward curiously to get a better view of his face.

'Is it your wife lying here?' she asked.

The painter made no reply.

'She must have been a good beautiful woman,' the old woman said. 'The Lord summoned her too soon.'

The painter shook his head.

'Not your wife?' the old woman asked. 'Is it your mother, then?'

'No,' the painter said. 'Not my mother. She's been dead for a long time.'

'Your father?'

'So has he,' the painter said.

Perplexed, the old woman glanced at the old tombstone, from the letters of which the rain had long since washed away the gold paint. 'My eyes are bad,' she said, 'and I've left my glasses at home. I am sorry.'

'Never mind,' the painter said. 'You don't need glasses in the cemetery.'

The old woman waddled closer and, wrinkling her forehead, tried to decipher the inscription.

'For an old woman like me it would be better if the Lord summoned her to his presence, believe you me! But you are still young, Comrade, you can have children!'

The painter made no reply.

'When the Lord takes one away, he can give you another instead,' said the old woman. Straining forward she continued to study the illegible inscription.

'I had a girl child myself ten years after my Joska!'

'Yes,' the painter said.

'Is it your son who is lying here?'

'No,' said the painter.

'Then it must be . . .'

'I've nobody lying here,' said the painter. 'I am mourning for mankind over a strange grave. I am a crazy artist, that's what I am.'

For a while the old woman remained silent, involuntarily tightening the black shawl round her shoulders. 'There's no need to mourn for that, my dear,' she said. 'It gets along all right. Well, God bless you, I am going home.'